Entering her room, Kel shut the door.
When she turned, a gasp escaped before
she locked her lips.

<hr />

She surveyed the damage. The narrow bed
was overturned. Mattress, sheets, and blankets
were strewn everywhere. The drapes lay on
the floor and the shutters hung open. Two
chairs, a bookcase, a pair of night tables, and
an oak clothespress were also upended. The
desk must have been too heavy for such treatment, but its drawers had been dumped onto
the floor. Her packs were opened and their
contents tumbled out. Someone had used her
practice glaive to slash and pull down the wall
hangings. On the plaster wall she saw written:
No Girls! Go Home! You Won't Last!

TAMORA PIERCE

FIRST TEST

BOOK 1 OF THE

Protector of the Small

QUARTET

To Mallory,
who totally made it happen

Published by Laurel-Leaf
an imprint of Random House Children's Books
a division of Random House, Inc.
New York

Originally published in hardcover in the United States by
Random House Books for Young Readers, New York, in 1999.
This edition published by arrangement with
Random House Books for Young Readers.

Laurel-Leaf and colophon are registered trademarks
of Random House, Inc.

www.randomhouse.com/teens
Educators and librarians, for a variety of teaching tools,
visit us at www.randomhouse.com/teachers

RL: 5.4
ISBN: 978-0-679-88917-5
January 2007
Printed in the United States of America
24 23 22 21 20

CONTENTS

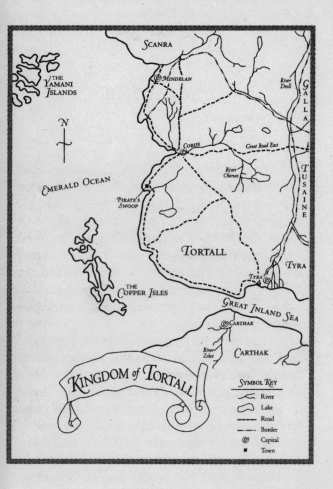

DECISIONS

*A*lanna the Lioness, the King's Champion, could hardly contain her glee. Baron Piers of Mindelan had written to King Jonathan to say that his daughter wished to be a page. Alanna fought to sit still as she watched Wyldon of Cavall, the royal training master, read the baron's letter. Seated across his desk from them, the king watched the training master as sharply as his Champion did. Lord Wyldon was known for his dislike of female warriors.

It had been ten long years since the proclamation that girls might attempt a page's training. Alanna had nearly given up hope that such a girl—or the kind of family that would allow her to do so—existed in Tortall, but at last she had come forward. Keladry of Mindelan would not have to hide her sex for eight years as Alanna had done. Keladry would prove to the world that girls could be knights. And she would not be friendless. Alanna had plans to help Keladry through the first few years. It never occurred to the Champion that anyone might object.

Alanna half turned to see Wyldon better. Surely he'd read the letter at least twice! From this side the puffy scars from his battle to save the younger princes and princess were starkly visible; Wyldon's right arm was in a sling yet from that fight. Alanna rubbed fingers that itched with the urge to apply healing magic. Wyldon had the idea that suffering pain made a warrior stronger. He would not thank her if she tried to heal him now.

Goddess bless, she thought tiredly. How will I ever get on with him if I'm to help this girl Keladry?

Wyldon was not flexible: he'd proved that to the entire court over and over. If he were any stiffer, Alanna thought wryly, I'd paint a design on him and use him for a shield. He's got no sense of humor and he rejects change just because it's change.

Still, she had to admit that his teaching worked. During the Immortals War of the spring and early summer, when legendary creatures had joined with the realm's human enemies to take the kingdom, the squires and pages had been forced into battle. They had done well, thanks to their training by Wyldon and the teachers he had picked.

At last Lord Wyldon returned the letter to King Jonathan, who placed it on his desk. "The baron and the baroness of Mindelan are faithful servants of the crown," the king remarked. "We would not have this treaty with the Yamani Islands were it not for them. You will have read that their daughter received some warrior training at the Yamani court, so it would appear that Keladry has an aptitude."

Lord Wyldon resettled his arm in its sling. "I did not agree to this, Your Majesty."

Alanna was about to say that he didn't have to agree when she saw the king give the tiniest shake of the head. Clenching her jaws, she kept her remark to herself as King Jonathan raised his eyebrows.

"Your predecessor agreed," he reminded Wyldon. "And you, my lord, implied agreement when you accepted the post of training master."

"That is a lawyer's reply, sire," Wyldon replied stiffly, a slight flush rising in his clean-shaven cheeks.

"Then here is a king's: we desire this girl to train as a page."

And that is that, Alanna thought, satisfied. She might be the kind of knight who would argue with her king, at least in private, but Wyldon would never let himself do so.

The training master absently rubbed the arm in its linen sling. At last he bowed in his chair. "May we compromise, sire?"

Alanna stiffened. She hated that word! "Com—" she began to say.

The king silenced her with a look. "What do you want, my lord?"

"In all honesty," said the training master, thinking aloud, "I had thought that our noble parents loved their daughters too much to place them in so hard a life."

"Not everyone is afraid to do anything new," Alanna replied sharply.

"Lioness," said the king, his voice dangerously quiet. Alanna clenched her fists. What was going on? Was Jonathan inclined to give way to the man who'd saved his children?

Wyldon's eyes met hers squarely. "Your bias is known, Lady Alanna." To the king he said, "Surely the girl's parents cannot be aware of the difficulties she will encounter."

"Baron Piers and Lady Ilane are not fools," replied King Jonathan. "They have given us three good, worthy knights already."

Lord Wyldon gave a reluctant nod. Anders, Inness, and Conal of Mindelan were credits to their training. The realm would feel the loss of Anders—whose war wounds could never heal entirely—from the active duty rolls. It would take years to replace those who were killed or maimed in the Immortals War.

"Sire, please, think this through," Wyldon said. "We need the realm's sons. Girls are fragile, more emotional, easier to frighten. They are not as strong in their arms and shoulders as men. They tire easily. This girl would get any warriors who serve with her killed on some dark night."

Alanna started to get up. This time King Jonathan walked out from behind his desk. Standing beside his Champion, he gripped one of her shoulders, keeping her in her chair.

"But I will be fair," Wyldon continued. His

brown eyes were hard. "Let her be on probation for a year. By the end of the summer field camp, if she has not convinced me of her ability to keep up, she must go home."

"Who judges her fitness?" inquired the king.

Wyldon's lips tightened. "Who but the training master, sire? I have the most experience in evaluating the young for their roles as future knights."

Alanna turned to stare at the king. "No boy has ever undergone a probationary period!" she cried.

Wyldon raised his good shoulder in a shrug. "Perhaps they should. For now, I will not tender my resignation over this, provided I judge whether this girl stays or goes in one year's time."

The king weighed the request. Alanna fidgeted. She knew Lord Wyldon meant his threat, and the crown needed him. Too many great nobles, dismayed by the changes in Tortall since Jonathan's coronation, felt that Wyldon was their voice at court. If he resigned, the king and queen would find it hard to get support for their future changes.

At last King Jonathan said, "Though we do not always agree, my lord, you know I respect you because you are fair and honorable. I would hate to see that fairness, that honor, tainted in any way. Keladry of Mindelan shall have a year's probation."

Lord Wyldon nodded, then inspected the nails on his good hand. "There is one other matter," he remarked slowly. He looked at Alanna. "Do you plan to involve yourself in the girl's training? It will not do."

Alanna bristled. "What is that supposed to mean?"

"You wish to help the girl, understandably." Wyldon spoke as though the mild words made his teeth hurt. "But you rarely deal with the lads, my lady. If you help the girl, it will be said that you eased her path in some special way. There are rumors that your successes are due to your magical Gift."

"By the Goddess," snapped Alanna, crimson with fury. If the king had not forbidden her to challenge men on personal grounds years before, she would have taken Wyldon out to the dueling court and made him regret his words.

"Alanna, for heaven's sake, you know the gossip," King Jonathan said. "Stop acting as if you'd never heard it before." He looked at Wyldon. "And you suggest…"

"Lady Alanna must keep from all contact with the girl," Wyldon replied firmly. "Even a moment's conversation will give rise to suspicion."

"All contact?" cried Alanna. "But she'll be the only girl among over twenty boys! She'll have questions—I could help—" She realized what she had said and fell silent.

King Jonathan gently patted her shoulder. "Is there no other way?" he asked.

Wyldon shook his head. "I fear not, sire. The Mindelan girl will be the cause of trouble as it is, without the Lioness hovering over her."

The king thought it over. At last he sighed. "Lord Wyldon has the right of it. You must stay away from Keladry of Mindelan, Alanna."

"But Jonathan—sire—" she pleaded, not believing he would do this.

"That is an order, lady knight. If you cannot accept that, say as much now, and I will find you work elsewhere."

She stared at him for a long moment, lips tight. At last she got to her feet. "Don't tax yourself. I'll find knight's work myself," she told him. "As far from Corus as possible." She stalked out of the room, slamming the door in her wake.

The men stared at the door. Each of them was trying to remember if Alanna the Lioness had ever spoken to Jonathan in that tone before.

*   *   *

Baron Piers and Lady Ilane of Mindelan watched Keladry read the reply from the training master. A Tortallan who did not know them well might have thought the man and woman felt nothing, and that their ten-year-old daughter was only concerned, not upset. That was far from true. The family had spent the last six years living in the Yamani Islands, where displays of deep emotion were regarded as shameful. To get the Yamanis to respect them, they had all learned to hide their feelings. Home in Mindelan again, they still acted as Yamanis, hiding uneasiness and even distress behind still faces.

Kel struggled to reread the letter, afraid to say

a word. If she did, her shaking voice would give her away. Instead she waited as she tried to control the anger and sense of betrayal that filled her.

"It is not the reply we expected," Baron Piers said at last. He was a short, stocky man. Keladry had his build, delicate nose, and dreamy, long-lashed hazel eyes. Her brown hair was several shades lighter than his. When Kel did not reply he continued, "His declaration of ten years ago was that girls could become pages. Nothing was said of probation then."

"Keladry?" asked her mother. "You can say what you feel. We are no longer among the Yamanis." She was a thin, elegant woman, taller than her husband by nearly a head, with hair that had gone white very early in life and a deep, musical voice. All Keladry had from her was height. At the age of ten the girl was already five feet tall and still growing.

It took Kel a moment to register what her mother had said. She tried a smile. "But, Mama, I don't want to get into bad habits, in case I go back with you." She looked at Lord Wyldon's letter again. She had expected to be a page when her parents returned to the Yamani Islands in eighteen months. From the tone of this letter, perhaps she ought not to count on that.

"It isn't right," she said quietly, even fiercely. "No boys have probation. I'm supposed to be treated the same."

"Don't give your answer yet," Baron Piers said quickly. "Take the letter with you. Think about what it says. You're not hasty, Kel—this is a bad time to start."

"Reflect as if you have all of time, even when time is short," added her mother in Yamani. "Be as stone."

Kel bowed Yamani-style, palms flat on her thighs. Then she went to find someplace quiet to think.

First she went to her room beside the nursery. That wasn't a good choice. Two of her brothers' young families lived at Mindelan. With the children and their nursemaids next door, there was enough noise to drown out trumpets. No one had seen her creep into the room, but her oldest nephew saw her leaving it. Nothing would do for him but that she give him a piggyback ride around the large room. After that, all of the older children wanted rides of their own. Once that was done, the nursemaids helped Kel to escape.

She tried to hole up by the fountain in the castle garden, but her sisters-in-law were there, sewing and gossiping with their maids. The kitchen garden was her next choice, but two servants were there gathering vegetables. She stared longingly at her favorite childhood spot, the highest tower in the castle, and felt a surge of anger. Before they had gone to the islands her brother Conal had teasingly held her over the edge of the tower balcony. Until that time she had visited the top of that tower at least once a day. Now the thought of it made her shudder.

There were hundreds of places she might use

around the castle, but they were all indoors. She needed to be outside. She was trying to think of a place when she remembered the broad, shallow Domin River, which ran through the woods. No one would be there. She could sit by the water and think in peace.

"Miss?" called a voice as she strode through the inner gate in the castle wall. "Where might you be going?"

Kel turned to face the man-at-arms who had called to her. "I don't know."

The man held out a small horn. "If you're not going to the village, you need one of these." He spoke carefully. The baron and his family had been home only for three months, and the people were still not sure what to make of these strange, Yamani-like nobles. "They told you the rule, surely. Any time you go outside the castle or village, you take a horn. You never know when one of them monsters, centaurs or giants or whatever, will show its face."

Kel frowned. The legendary creatures that had returned to their world five years before had an unnerving way of showing up when they were least expected. For every one that was harmless or willing to get on with humans, there were fistfuls that weren't. Bands of men-at-arms now roamed throughout the fiefdom, searching for hostile visitors and listening for the horn call, which meant someone was in trouble.

I'm not going very far, she wanted to argue, but the Yamanis had taught her to obey a soldier's commands. She accepted the horn with a quiet thank-you and slung it over one shoulder. Checking that Lord Wyldon's letter was tucked securely in the front of her shirt, she left the road that led from the castle gate and headed through their orchards. Once past the cultivated trees she entered the woods, following a trail down to the water.

By the time she could see a glint of silver through the trees she had worked up a mild sweat. The day was warm and the walk was longer than she had thought it would be. When a rock worked its way into her shoe, she sat on a log to get it out.

"It's not right," she muttered to herself, undoing the laces that held the leather around her ankle. "You're a page for four years. That's how it's been done for centuries. Now they're going to change it?" When she up-ended the shoe and shook it, nothing fell out. She stuffed a hand inside, feeling around for the stone. "And just because I'm a girl? They ought to treat me the same. All I want is the same chance as the boys. No more, no less. That's right, isn't it?" She winced as a sharp edge nipped one of her fingers. Working more carefully, she wiggled the bit of rock out of a fold in the leather. "Probation is not fair, and knighthood training has to be fair."

The stone was out; her mind was made up. If they couldn't treat her the same as they would the boys, then she wasn't going to settle for a half portion. She would have to become a warrior some other way.

Kel sighed and put her shoe back on. The problem was that now she would have to wait. The Queen's Riders took volunteers when they were fifteen or older. The queen's ladies, those who were expected to ride, handle a bow, and deal with trouble at Queen Thayet's side, went to her in their fifteenth year as well. And who was to say Kel wouldn't be living in the Yamani Islands by then?

One thing she knew: convent school, the normal destination for noble girls her age, was not a choice. Kel had no interest whatever in ladylike arts, and even less interest in the skills needed to attract a husband or manage a castle. Even if she did, who would have her? Once she'd overheard her sisters-in-law comment that no man would be interested in a girl who was built along the lines of a cow.

She'd made the mistake of repeating that comment to her mother, when Kel's plan to be a page had first come up. Her mother had gone white with fury and had put her daughters-in-law to mending several years' worth of old linens. It had taken a great deal of persuasion for Kel to convince her mother that her quest for knighthood did not mean she wanted to settle for second best, knowing she would never marry. Getting Ilane of Mindelan to agree to her being a page had been a negotiation every bit as complicated as what her father had done to get the Yamanis to sign the treaty.

And see the good that did me, Kel thought

with disgust. Lord Wyldon offers me second best anyway, and I won't take it. I could have saved my breath talking Mama around.

She was ready to get to her feet when the sound of bodies crashing through the brush made her look up. Gruff voices reached her ear.

"Hurry up!" a boy growled from near the river. "Do you want us t'get caught?"

"The Cow's at home," replied a second boy's voice. "She stays there all morning."

Kel stood, listening. If they were on the look-out for her, then they were up to something bad. In just three months she had taught the local boys she was someone to respect. Kel grabbed a sturdy fallen branch and ran toward the voices. Racing into open ground between the trees and river, she saw three village boys. They were about to throw a wriggling cloth sack into the Domin.

Her mouth settled into a tight, angry line; her hazel eyes glittered. "Put that down!" she cried.

The boys whirled, startled, dropping their burden on a half-submerged tree limb. One of them punched the smallest in the shoulder. "Home all morning, eh?"

Kel shouted, "I know all of you! And you know the law in Mindelan—no killing of animals without the baron's leave!"

The biggest, taller than she by half a head, advanced. The other two were right behind him. "Who's to make us stop, Cow?"

The Yamanis had taught her well. She waded into the boys, using her club as an equalizer. She whacked them in the belly so they couldn't breathe, and on the collarbones and biceps so they couldn't raise their arms. One youth punched her face; he caught her on the outside of one eye. She changed her grip on her branch and swept his feet from under him, then stood on one of his arms.

Another lad grabbed a branch and swung at her; she blocked it with hers, then rammed the length of wood into his stomach. He doubled over, gasping. Kel shoved him into the third boy. Down they went in a tumble. When they untangled themselves, they ran. Their comrade also chose to make his escape.

Kel looked around for the sack. The current had tugged the tree limb on which it rested out into the deeper, faster water at the center of the river. She didn't hesitate, but waded into the water. Kel was a good swimmer and the river here was fairly shallow. She doubted that whatever small creatures were struggling in the sack could swim.

Movement on the far bank made her look up. What she saw made her halt, cold water rushing around her thighs. Something black and strange-looking walked out from under the shelter of the trees. It looked like a giant furred spider nearly five feet tall, with one difference. The thing had a human head. It stared at Kel, then grinned broadly to reveal sharp teeth.

Her flesh crawled; hairs stood up on her arms and the back of her neck. Spidren, she thought, recognizing it from descriptions. Spidrens in our woods.

Like most of the legendary creatures that now prowled the human realms, they were virtually immortal, immune to disease and old age. They died only when something or someone took pains to kill them. They fed on animals and human blood. No one could get spidrens to make peace with human beings.

The thing reared up on its back legs, revealing a light-colored shaft at the base of its belly. From it the spidren squirted a high-flying gray stream that soared into the air over the river. Kel threw herself to one side, away from the gray stream and the sack she was trying to catch. The stuff was like rope. She realized it was a web when it fell in a long line across the surface of the water. It had missed her by only a foot. The spidren bent and snipped the rope off from its belly spinneret with a clawed leg. Swiftly it began to wind the length of web around another clawed foot. As it dragged through the water, the sticky thing caught on the cloth sack. The spidren reeled in its catch as a fisherman might pull in a line.

Kel brought the horn up to her mouth. She blew five hard blasts and might have continued to blow until help came, as the spidren gathered up the sack. It discarded its web with one clawed foot, held the sack with a second, and reached into it with a third. The beast grinned, its eyes never leaving Kel, as it pulled out a wet and squirming kitten.

The horn fell from the girl's lips as the spidren looked the kitten over. It smacked its lips, then bit the small creature in half and began to chew.

Kel screamed and groped on the river bottom with both hands for ammunition. Coming up with a stone in each fist, she hurled the first. It soared past the spidren, missing by inches. Her next stone caught it square in the head. It shrieked and began to climb the bluff that overlooked the river to its left, still holding the sack.

In the distance Kel heard the sound of horns. Help was on its way—for her, but not for those kittens. She scrabbled for more stones and plunged across the river, battling the water to get to the same shore as the monster. It continued to climb the rocky face of the bluff until it reached the summit just as Kel scrambled onto the land.

Once she was on solid ground, she began to climb the bluff, her soaked feet digging for purchase in soft dirt and rock. Above, the spidren leaned over the edge of the bluff to leer at her. It reached into the sack, dragged out a second kitten, and began to eat it.

Kel still had a rock in her right hand. She hurled it as hard as she had ever thrown a ball to knock down a target. It smashed the spidren's nose. The thing shrieked and hissed, dropping the rest of its meal.

Kel's foot slipped. She looked down to find a better place to set it and froze. She was only seven feet above the water, but the distance seemed more like seventy to her. A roar filled her ears and her head spun. Cold sweat trickled through her clothes. She clung to the face of the bluff with both arms and legs, sick with fear.

Leaving its sack on the ground, the spidren threw a loop of web around a nearby tree stump. When it was set, the creature began to lower itself over the side of the bluff. Its hate-filled eyes were locked on the girl, whose terror had frozen her in place.

Kel was deaf and blind to the spidren's approach. Later she could not recall hearing the monster's scream as arrows thudded into its flesh, just as she could not remember the arrival of her brother Anders and his men-at-arms.

With the spidren's death, its web rope snapped. The thing hurtled past Kel to splash into the river.

A man-at-arms climbed up to get her, gently prying her clutching fingers from their holds. Only when Kel was safely on the shore, seated on a flat rock, was she able to tell them why she had tried to kill a spidren with only stones for weapons. Someone climbed the bluff to retrieve the sack of kittens while Kel stared, shivering, at the spidren's body.

Her brother Anders dismounted stiffly and limped over to her. Reaching into his belt-pouch, he pulled out a handful of fresh mint leaves, crushed them in one gloved hand, and held them under Kel's nose. She breathed their fresh scent in gratefully.

"You're supposed to have real weapons when you go after something that's twice as big as you are," he told her mildly. "Didn't the Yamanis teach you that?" During the years most of their family had been in the Islands, Anders, Inness, and Conal, the three oldest sons of the manor, had served the crown as pages, squires, then knights. All they knew of Kel's experiences there came in their family's letters.

"I had to do something," Kel explained.

"Calling for help and staying put would have been wiser," he pointed out. "Leave the fighting to real warriors. Here we are." A man-at-arms put the recovered sack into his hands. Anders in turn put the bag in Kel's lap.

Nervously she pulled the bag open. Five wet kittens, their eyes barely opened, turned their faces up to her and protested their morning's adventure. "I'll take you to our housekeeper," Kel promised them. "She knows what to do with kittens."

Once the animals were seen to and she had changed into a clean gown and slippers, Kel went to her father's study. With her came a small group of animals: two elderly dogs, three cats, two puppies, a kitten, and a three-legged pine marten. Kel gently moved them out of the way and closed the door before they could sneak into the room. Anders was there, leaning on a walking stick as he talked to their parents. All three adults fell silent and looked at Kel.

"I'll do it," she said quietly. "I want the training, and the right weapons. Anders was right. It was stupid to go after a spidren with stones."

"And if they send you home at the end of a year?" asked Ilane of Mindelan.

Kel took a deep breath. "Then I'll still know more than I do now," she said firmly.

Piers looked at his wife, who nodded. "Then we'd best pack," said Ilane, getting to her feet. "You leave the day after tomorrow." Passing Kel on her way to the door, her mother lightly touched the eye the village boy had hit. It was red, blue, and puffy—not the worst black eye Kel had ever gotten. "Let's also get a piece of raw meat to put on this," suggested the woman.

The next evening, Kel made her way to the stables to visit her pony, Chipper, to explain to him that the palace would supply her with a knight's mount. The pony lipped her shirt in an understanding way. He at least would be in good hands: Anders's oldest son was ready to start riding, and he loved the pony.

"I thought I might find you here," a voice said as Kel fed Chip an apple. She squeaked in surprise. For a man with a limp and a cane, Anders moved very quietly. "You know we'll take care of him."

Kel nodded and picked up a brush to groom the pony's round sides. "I know. I'll miss him all the same."

Anders leaned against a post. "Kel..."

She looked at him. Since the incident on the river the day before, she'd caught Anders watching her. She barely remembered him before their departure to the Islands, six years ago—he had already been a knight, handsome and distant in his armor, always riding somewhere. In the months since their return to Mindelan, she had come to like him. "Something the matter?" she asked.

Anders sighed. "Do you realize it's going to be hard? Maybe impossible? They'll make it tough. There's hazing, for one thing. I don't know when the custom started, but it's called 'earning your way.' It's just for the first-year pages. The senior ones make you run stupid little errands, like fetching gloves and picking up things that get knocked over. You have to do it. Otherwise it's the same as saying you don't have to do what the older pages did, as if you think you're better than they are. And older pages play tricks on the young ones, and some of them will pick fights. Stand up for yourself, or they'll make your life a misery."

"In the rules they sent, fighting isn't allowed."

"Of course it's forbidden. If you're caught, they punish you. That's expected. What you must never do is tattle on another page, or say who you fought with. That's expected, too. Tell them you fell down—that's what I always said. Otherwise no one will trust you. A boy told when I was a page. He finally left because no one would speak to him."

"But they'll punish me for fighting?"

"With chores, extra lessons, things like that. You take every punishment, whatever it's for, and keep quiet."

"Like the Yamanis," she said, brushing loose hairs from Chipper's coat. "You don't talk—you obey."

Anders nodded. "Just do what you're told. Don't complain. If you can't do it, say that you failed, not that you can't. No one can finish every task that's given. What your teachers don't want is excuses, or blaming someone else, or saying it's unfair. They know it's unfair. Do what you can, and take your punishment in silence."

Kel nodded. "I can do that, I think."

Anders chuckled. "That's the strange thing— I believe you can. But, Kel—"

Kel went to Chip's far side, looking at Anders over the pony's back. "What?"

The young man absently rubbed his stiff leg. "Kel, all these things you learned in the Islands..."

"Yes?" she prodded when he fell silent again.

"You might want to keep them to yourself. Otherwise, the pages might think you believe you're better than they are. You don't want to be different, all right? At least, not any more different than you already are."

"Won't they want to learn new things?" she wanted to know. "I would."

"Not everyone's like you, Kel. Do what they teach you, no more. You'll save yourself heartache that way."

Kel smiled. "I'll try," she told him.

Anders straightened with a wince. "Don't be out here too long," he reminded her. "You're up before dawn."

Unlike normal dreams, in which time and places and people did strange things, this dream was completely true to Kel's memory. It began as she knelt before an altar and stared at the swords placed on it. The weapons were sheathed in pure gold rubbed as smooth and bright as glass. She was five years old again.

"They are the swords given to the children of the fire goddess, Yama," a lady-in-waiting beside Kel said, awe in her soft voice. "The short sword is the sword of law. Without it, we are only animals. The long sword is the sword of duty. It is the terrible sword, the killing sword." Her words struck a chord in Kel that left the little girl breathless. She liked the idea that duty was a killing sword. "Without duty," the lady continued, "duty to our lords, to our families, and to the law, we are less than animals."

Kel smelled burning wood. She looked around, curious. The large oil lamps that hung from the temple ceiling by thick cords smelled of perfume, not wood. Kel sniffed the air. She knew that fires were terrible on the Yamani Islands, where indoor walls were often paper screens and straw mats covered floors of polished wood.

The lady-in-waiting got to her feet.

The temple doors crashed open. There was Kel's mother, Ilane, her outer kimono flapping open, her thick pale hair falling out of its pins. In her hands she carried a staff capped with a broad, curved blade. Her blue-green eyes were huge in her bone-white face.

"Please excuse me," she told the lady-in-waiting, as calm and polite as any Yamani in danger, "but we must get out of here and find help. Pirates have attacked the cove and are within the palace."

There was a thunder of shod feet on polished wood floors. Swords and axes crashed through the paper screens that formed the wall behind the altar. Scanrans—men already covered in blood and grime—burst into the room, fighting their way clear of the screens and their wooden frames.

An arm wrapped tight around Kel's ribs, yanking her from her feet. The lady-in-waiting had scooped her up in one arm and the swords in the other. Faster than the raiders she ran to Ilane of Mindelan.

The lady tumbled to the ground. Kel slid out the door on her belly. Turning, too startled to cry, she saw the lady at her mother's feet. There was an arrow in the Yamani woman's back.

Ilane bent over the dead woman and took the swords. Hoisting them in one hand, she swung her weapon to her right and to her left. It sheared through the heavy cords that suspended five large oil lamps. They fell and shattered, spilling a flood of burning oil. It raced across the temple in the path of the raiders who were running toward them. When their feet began to burn, they halted, trying to put the fire out.

"Come on!" Kel's mother urged. "Hike up those skirts and run!"

Kel yanked her kimono up and fled with Ilane. They skidded and slipped over the polished floors in their Yamani sock-shoes, then turned down one corridor and another. Far down one passage they saw a new group of Scanrans. Kel and her mother ran around a corner. They tried another turning—it led to a dead end. They were trapped. The walls that now blocked them in on three sides were sturdy wood, too. They could have cut their way through paper ones.

Ilane turned. Scanrans armed with swords or axes blocked the way out.

Ilane thrust the gold swords into Kel's arms and pushed her into a corner, then stood before her. "Get down and be quiet!" she said, gripping her weapon in both hands. "I think I can hold them off with this."

Kel put the swords behind her and huddled. The men came at her mother, laughing and joking in Scanran. She peeked around the edge of her mother's kimono. At that moment Ilane swung the bladed staff—glaive, Kel remembered as it swung, they called it a glaive—in a wide side cut, slicing one pirate across the chest. Whipping it back to her left, she caught another of them in the throat. Blood struck Kel's face; even dreaming, she could smell it. Breathless, the sheathed swords poking into her back, she watched her mother lunge and retreat, using her skill and her longer weapon to hold the enemy off. Ilane killed a third and a fourth attacker before a squad of guardsmen raced around the corner to finish the rest.

When the pirates were dead, Kel's mother turned and reached a hand down to her. "Let's go find your father," she said quietly.

Kel grasped the hand, and let her mother pull her to her feet. Then Kel gathered up the golden swords that had been trusted to them.

When they faced their rescuers, the guards knelt as one. They bowed low to the woman and the girl, touching their heads to the bloody floor.

Kel woke, breathing fast, her eyes shining. Her heart raced; she trembled all over. The dream was not scary; it was exciting. She loved it. She loved that it had all been real.

I want to be like that, she told herself as she always did. I want to protect people. And I will. I will. I'll be a hero one day, just like Mama. Just like the Lioness.

Nobody will kill two kittens in front of me then.

two

NOT SO WELCOME

Wyldon of Cavall nodded to Baron Piers, but his eyes were on Kel. He looked her over from top to toe, taking in every wrinkle and spot in her tunic and breeches and the fading bruise around her eye.

Kel met his gaze squarely. The training master was handsome, for all that he was completely bald on top. He wore what was left of his light brown hair cropped very short. A scar—so red and puffy, it had to be recent—ran from the corner of his eye across his right temple to dig a track through his hair to his ear. His right arm rested in a sling. His eyes were brown, his mouth wide; his chin was square with a hint of a cleft in it. His big hands were marked with scars. He dressed simply, in a pale blue tunic, a white shirt, and dark blue hose. She couldn't see his feet behind the big desk, but she suspected that his shoes were as sensible as the rest of him.

Even the Yamanis would say he's got too much stone in him, she thought, looking at the scuffed toes of her boots. He needs water to balance his nature. Peering through her lashes at the training master, she added, *Lots* of water. A century or two of it, maybe.

Wyldon drummed his fingers on his desktop. At last he smiled tightly. "Be seated, please, both of you."

Kel and her father obeyed.

Wyldon took his own seat. "Well. Keladry, is it?" She nodded. "You understand that you are here on sufferance. You have a year in which to prove that you can keep up with the boys. If you do not satisfy me on that count, you will go home."

He's never said that to any boy, Kel thought, glad that her face would not show her resentment. He shouldn't be saying it to me. She kept her voice polite as she answered, "Yes, my lord."

"You will get no special privileges or treatment, despite your sex." Wyldon's eyes were stony. "I will not tolerate flirtations. If there is a boy in your room, the door must be open. The same is true if you are in a boy's room. Should you disobey, you will be sent home immediately."

Kel met his eyes. "Yes, sir." She was talkative enough with her family, but not with outsiders. The chill that rose from Wyldon made her even quieter.

Piers shifted in his seat. "My daughter is only ten, Lord Wyldon. She's a bit young for that kind of thing."

"My experience with females is that they begin early," the training master said flatly. He ran a blunt-tipped finger down a piece of paper.

"It says here that you claim no magical Gift," stated Lord Wyldon. "Is that so?"

Kel nodded.

Lord Wyldon put down the paper and leaned forward, clasping his hands on his neatly ordered desk. "In your father's day, the royal household always dined in the banquet hall. Now our royal family dines privately for the most part. On great holidays and on special occasions, feasts are held with the sovereigns, nobles, and guests in attendance. The pages are required to serve at such banquets. Also, you are required to run errands for any lord or lady who asks.

"Has she a servant with her?" he asked Kel's father.

"No," Piers replied.

"Very well. Palace staff will tend her rooms. Have you any questions?" Wyldon asked Kel.

Yes, she wanted to say. Why won't you treat me like you treat the boys? Why can't you be *fair*?

She kept it to herself. Growing up in a diplomat's house, she had learned how to read people. A good look at Wyldon's square, stubborn face with its hard jaw had told Kel that words would mean nothing to this man. She would have to prove to him that she was as good as any boy. And she would.

"No questions, my lord," she told him quietly.

"There is a chamber across the hall for your farewells," Wyldon told Piers. "Salma will come for Keladry and guide her to her assigned room.

No doubt her baggage already is there." He looked at Kel. "Unpack your things neatly. When the supper bell rings, stand in the hall with the new boys. Sponsors—older pages who show the new ones how things are done—must be chosen before we go down to the mess."

After Kel said goodbye to her father, she found Salma waiting for her in the hall. The woman was short and thin, with frizzy brown hair and large, dark eyes. She wore the palace uniform for women servants, a dark skirt and a white blouse. A large ring laden with keys hung from her belt. As she took Kel to her new room, Salma asked if Kel had brought a personal servant.

When the girl replied that she hadn't, Salma told her, "In that case, I'll assign a servant to you. We bring you hot water for washup and get your fire going in the morning. We also do your laundry and mending, make beds, sweep, and so on. And if you play any tricks on the servants, you'll do your laundry and bed-making for the rest of the year. It's not our job to look after weapons, equipment, or armor, mind. That's what you're here to learn."

She briskly led the way through one long hall as she talked. Now they passed a row of doors. Each bore a piece of slate with a name written in chalk. "That's my room," Salma explained, pointing. "The ground floor here is the pages' wing. Squires are the next floor up. If you need supplies, or special cleaning and sewing, or if you are ill, come to me."

Kel looked at her curiously. "My brothers didn't mention you."

"Timon Greendale, our headman, reorganized service here six years ago," Salma replied. "I was brought in five years back—just in time to meet your brother Conal. Don't worry. I won't hold it against you."

Kel smiled wryly. Conal had that effect on people.

Salma halted in front of the last door in the hall. There was no name written on the slate. "This is your room," she remarked. "I told the men to put your things here." She brushed the slate with her fingertips. "Your name has been washed off. I have to get my chalk. You may as well unpack."

"Thank you," Kel said.

"No need to thank me" was Salma's calm reply. "I do what they pay me to." She hesitated, then added, "If you need anything, even if it's just a sympathetic ear, tell me." She rested a warm hand on Kel's shoulder for a moment, then walked away.

Entering her room, Kel shut the door. When she turned, a gasp escaped before she locked her lips.

She surveyed the damage. The narrow bed was overturned. Mattress, sheets, and blankets were strewn everywhere. The drapes lay on the floor and the shutters hung open. Two chairs, a bookcase, a pair of night tables, and an oak clothespress were also upended. The desk must have been too heavy for such treatment, but its drawers had been dumped onto the floor. Her packs were opened and their contents tumbled out. Someone had used her practice glaive to slash and pull down the wall hangings. On the plaster wall she saw written: *No Girls! Go Home! You Won't Last!*

Kel took deep breaths until the storm of hurt and anger that filled her was under control. Once that was done, she began to clean up. The first thing she checked was the small wooden box containing her collection of Yamani porcelain lucky cats. She had a dozen or so, each a different size and color, each sitting with one paw upraised. The box itself was dented on one corner, but its contents were safe. Her mother had packed each cat in a handkerchief to keep it from breaking.

That's something, at least, Kel thought. But what about next time? Maybe she ought to ship them home.

As she gathered up her clothes, she heard a knock. She opened her door a crack. It was Salma. The minute the woman saw her face, she knew something was wrong. "Open," she commanded.

Kel let her in and shut the door.

"You were warned this kind of thing might happen?" Salma asked finally.

Kel nodded. "I'm cleaning up."

"I told you, it's your job to perform a warrior's tasks. *We* do this kind of work," Salma replied. "Leave this to me. By the time you come back from supper it will be as good as new. Are you going to change clothes?"

Kel nodded.

"Why don't you do that? It's nearly time for you to wait outside. I'll need your key once you're done in here."

Kel scooped up the things she needed and walked into the next room. Small and bare, it served as a dressing room and bathroom. The privy was behind a door set in the wall. There was little in here to destroy, but the mirror and the privy seat were soaped.

Kel shut the door. Before she had seen her room, she had planned to wear tunic and breeches as she had for the journey. She'd thought that if she was to train as a boy, she ought to dress like one. They were also more comfortable. Now she felt differently. She was a girl; she had nothing to be ashamed of, and they had better learn *that* first thing. The best way to remind them was to dress at least part of the time as a girl.

Stripping off her travel-stained clothes, she pulled on a yellow linen shift and topped it with her second-best dress, a fawn-brown cotton that looked well against the yellow. She removed her boots and put on white stockings and brown leather slippers.

Cleaning the mirror, she looked at herself. The gown was creased from being packed, but that could not be helped. She still had a black eye. There was nothing she could do with her mouse-brown hair: she'd had it cropped to her earlobes before she'd left home. Next trip to market, maybe I'll get some ribbons, she thought grimly, running a comb through her hair. Some nice, bright ribbons.

She grinned at her own folly. Hadn't she learned by now that the first thing a boy grabbed in a fight was hair? She'd lose chunks of it or get half choked if she wore ornaments and ribbons.

Overhead a bell clanged three times. She winced: the sound was *loud*.

"Time," Salma called.

If she thought anything of the change in Kel's appearance, she kept it to herself. Instead she pointed to yet another piece of writing: *Girls Can't Fight!* Salma's mouth twisted wryly. "What do they think their mothers do, when the lords are at war and a raiding party strikes? Stay in their solars and tat lace?"

That made Kel smile. "My aunt lit barrels of lard and had them catapulted onto Scanran ships this summer."

"As would any delicately reared noblewoman." Salma opened the door. Once they had walked into the hall, she took the key from Kel and went about her business, nodding to the boys as they emerged from their rooms.

Kel stood in front of her door and clasped her hands so no one could see they shook. Suddenly she wanted to turn tail and run until she reached home.

Wyldon was coming down the hall. Boys joined him as he passed, talking quietly. One of them was a boy with white-blond hair and blue eyes, set in a face as rosy-cheeked as a girl's. Kel, seeing the crispness of his movements and a stubbornness around his mouth, guessed that anybody silly enough to mistake that one for a girl would be quickly taught his mistake. A big, cheerful-looking redheaded boy walked on Wyldon's left, joking with a very tall, lanky youth.

A step behind the blond page and Wyldon came a tall boy who walked with a lion's arrogance. He was brown-skinned and black-eyed, his nose proudly arched. A Bazhir tribesman from the southern desert, Kel guessed. She noticed several other Bazhir among the pages, but none looked as kingly as this one.

When the training master halted, there were only five people left in front of doors on both sides of him: four boys and Kel. Her next-door neighbor, a brown-haired boy liberally sprinkled with freckles, bowed to Wyldon. Kel and the others did the same; then Kel wondered if she ought to have curtsied. She let it go. To do so now, after bowing, would just make her look silly.

Wyldon looked at each of them in turn, his eyes resting the longest on Kel. "Don't think you'll have an easy time this year. You will work hard. You'll work when you're tired, when you're ill, and when you think you can't possibly work anymore. You have one more day to laze. Your sponsor will show you around this palace and collect those things which the crown supplies to you. The day after that, we begin."

"You." He pointed to a boy with the reddest, straightest hair Kel had ever seen. "Your name and the holding of your family."

The boy stammered, "Merric, sir—my lord. Merric of Hollyrose." He had pale blue eyes and a long, broad nose; his skin had only the barest summer tan.

The training master looked at the pages around him. "Which of you older pages will sponsor Merric and teach him our ways?"

"Please, Lord Wyldon?" Kel wasn't able to see the owner of the voice in the knot of boys who stood at Wyldon's back. "We're kinsmen, Merric and I."

"And kinsmen should stick together. Well said, Faleron of King's Reach." A handsome, dark-haired boy came to stand with Merric, smiling at the redhead. Wyldon pointed to the freckled lad, Esmond of Nicoline, who was taken into the charge of Cleon of Kennan, the big redhead. Blond, impish Quinden of Marti's Hill was sponsored by the regal-looking Bazhir, Zahir ibn Alhaz. The next pairing was the most notable: Crown Prince Roald, the twelve-year-old heir to the throne, chose to show Seaver of Tasride around. Seaver, whose dark complexion and coal-black eyes and hair suggested Bazhir ancestors, stared at Roald nervously, but relaxed when the prince rested a gentle hand on his shoulder.

Only Kel remained. Wyldon demanded, "Your name and your fief?"

She gulped. "Keladry of Mindelan."

"Who will sponsor her?" asked Wyldon.

The handsome Zahir looked at her and sniffed. "Girls have no business in the affairs of men. This one should go home." He glared at Kel, who met his eyes calmly.

Lord Wyldon shook his head. "We are not among the Bazhir tribes, Zahir ibn Alhaz. Moreover, I requested a sponsor, not an opinion." He looked at the other boys. "Will no one offer?" he asked. "No beginner may go unsponsored."

"Look at her," Kel heard a boy murmur. "She stands there like—like a *lump*."

The blond youth at Wyldon's side raised a hand. "May I, my lord?" he asked.

Lord Wyldon stared at him. "You, Joren of Stone Mountain?"

The youth bowed. "I would be pleased to teach the girl all she needs to know of life in the pages' wing."

Kel eyed him, suspicious. From the way a few older pages giggled, she suspected Joren might plan to chase her away, not show her around. She looked at the training master, expecting him to agree with the blond page.

Instead Lord Wyldon frowned. "I had hoped for another sponsor," he commented stiffly. "You should employ your spare hours in the improvement of your classwork and your riding skills."

"I thought Joren hated—" someone whispered.

"Shut up!" another boy hissed.

Kel looked at the flagstones under her feet.

Now she was fighting to hide her embarrassment, but she knew she was failing. Any Yamani would see her shame on her features. She clasped her hands before her and schooled her features to smoothness. I'm a rock, she thought. I am stone.

"I believe I can perfect my studies and sponsor the girl," Joren said respectfully. "And since I am the only volunteer—"

"I suppose I'm being rash and peculiar, *again*," someone remarked in a drawling voice, "but if it means helping my friend Joren improve his studies, well, I'll just have to sacrifice myself. There's nothing I won't do to further the cause of book learning among my peers."

Everyone turned toward the speaker, who stood at the back of the group. Seeing him clearly, Kel thought that he was too old to be a page. He was tall, fair-skinned, and lean, with emerald eyes and light brown hair that swept back from a widow's peak.

Lord Wyldon absently rubbed the arm he kept tucked in a sling. "You volunteer, Nealan of Queenscove?"

The youth bowed jerkily. "That I do, your worship, sir." There was the barest hint of a taunt in Nealan's educated voice.

"A sponsor should be a page in his second year at least," Wyldon informed Nealan. "And you will mind your tongue."

"I know I only joined this little band in April, your lordship," the youth Nealan remarked cheerily, "but I have lived at court almost all of my fifteen years. I know the palace and its ways. And unlike Joren, I need not worry about my academics."

Kel stared at the youth. Had he always been mad, or did a few months under Wyldon do this to him? She had just arrived, and *she* knew better than to bait the training master.

Wyldon's eyebrows snapped together. "You have been told to mind your manners, Page Nealan. I will have an apology for your insolence."

Nealan bowed deeply. "An apology for general insolence, your lordship, or some particular offense?"

"One week scrubbing pots," ordered Lord Wyldon. "Be silent."

Nealan threw out an arm like a player making a dramatic statement. "How can I be silent and yet apologize?"

"*Two* weeks." Keladry was forgotten as Wyldon concentrated on the green-eyed youth. "The first duty for anyone in service to the crown is obedience."

"And I am a terrible obeyer," retorted Nealan. "All these inconvenient arguments spring to my mind, and I just have to make them."

"Three," Wyldon said tightly.

"Neal, shut it!" someone whispered.

"I could learn—" Kel squeaked. No one heard. She cleared her throat and repeated, "I can learn it on my own."

The boys turned to stare. Wyldon glanced at her. "What did you say?"

"I'll find my way on my own," Kel repeated. "Nobody has to show me. I'll probably learn better, poking around." She knew that wasn't the case—her father had once referred to the palace as a "miserable rat-warren"—but she couldn't let this mad boy get himself deeper into trouble on her account.

Nealan stared at her, winged brows raised.

"When I require your opinion," began Wyldon, his dark eyes snapping.

"It's no trouble," Nealan interrupted. "None at all, Demoiselle Keladry. My lord, I apologize for my wicked tongue and dreadful manners. I shall do my best not to encourage her to follow my example."

Wyldon, about to speak, seemed to think better of what he meant to say. He waited a moment, then said, "You are her sponsor, then. Now. Enough time has been wasted on foolishness. Supper."

He strode off, pages following like ducklings in their mother's wake. When the hall cleared, only Nealan and Keladry were left.

Nealan stared at the girl, his slanting eyes taking her in. Seeing him up close at last, Kel noticed that he had a willful face, with high cheekbones and arched brows. "Believe me, you wouldn't have liked Joren as a sponsor," Nealan informed her. "He'd drive you out in a week. With me at least you might last a while, even if I am at the bottom of Lord Wyldon's list. Come on." He strode off.

Kel stayed where she was. Halfway down the

hall, Nealan realized she was not behind him. When he turned and saw her still in front of her room, he sighed gustily, and beckoned. Kel remained where she was.

Finally he stomped back to her. "What part of 'come on' was unclear, page?"

"Why do you care if I last a week or longer?" she demanded. "Queenscove is a ducal house. Mindelan's just a barony, and a new one at that. Nobody cares about Mindelan. We aren't related, and our fathers aren't friends. So who am I to you?"

Nealan stared at her. "Direct little thing, aren't you?"

Kel crossed her arms over her chest and waited. The talkative boy didn't seem to have much patience. He would wear out before she did in a waiting contest.

Nealan sighed and ran his fingers through his hair. "Look—you heard me say I've lived at court almost all my life, right?"

Kel nodded.

"Well, think about that. I've lived at court and my father's the chief of the realm's healers. I've spent time with the queen and quite a few of the Queen's Riders and the King's Champion. I've watched Lady Alanna fight for the crown. I saw her majesty and some of her ladies fight in the Immortals War. I know women can be warriors. If that's the life you want, then you ought to have the same chance to get it as anyone else who's here." He stopped, then shook his head with a rueful smile. "I keep forgetting I'm not in a university debate. Sorry about the speech. Can we go eat now?"

Kel nodded again. This time, when he strode off down the hall, she trotted to keep up with him.

When they passed through an intersection of halls, Nealan pointed. "Note that stairwell. Don't let anyone tell you it's a shortcut to the mess or the classrooms. It heads straight down and ends on the lower levels, underground."

"Yessir."

"Don't call me sir."

"Yessir."

Nealan halted. "Was that meant to be funny?"

"Nossir," Kel replied, happy to stop and catch her breath. Nealan walked as he spoke, briskly.

Nealan threw up his hands and resumed his course. Finally they entered a room filled with noise. To Kel it seemed as if every boy in the world was here, yelling and jostling around rows of long tables and benches. She came to a halt, but Nealan beckoned her to follow. He led her to stacks of trays, plates, napkins, and cutlery, grabbing what he needed. Copying him, Kel soon had a bowl of a soup thick with leeks and barley, big slices of ham, a crusty roll still hot from the oven, and saffron rice studded with raisins and almonds. She had noticed pitchers of liquids, bowls of fruit, honey pots, and platters of cheese were already on the tables.

As they stopped, looking for a place to sit, the

racket faded. Eyes turned their way. Within seconds she could hear the whispers. "Look." "The Girl." "It's *her*." One clear voice exclaimed, "Who cares? She won't last."

Kel bit her lip and stared at her tray. Stone, she thought in Yamani. I am stone.

Nealan gave no sign of hearing, but marched toward seats at the end of one table. As they sat across from one another, the boys closest to them moved. Two seats beside Nealan were left empty, and three next to Kel.

"This is nice," Nealan remarked cheerfully. He put his food on the table before him and shoved his tray into the gap between him and the next boy. "Usually it's impossible to get a bit of elbow room here."

Someone rapped on a table. Lord Wyldon stood alone at a lectern in front of the room. The boys and Kel got to their feet as Wyldon raised his hands. "To Mithros, god of warriors and of truth, and to the Great Mother Goddess, we give thanks for their bounty," he said.

"We give thanks and praise," responded his audience.

"We ask the guidance of Mithros in these uncertain times, when change threatens all that is time-honored and true. May the god's light show us a path back to the virtues of our fathers and an end to uncertain times. We ask this of Mithros, god of the sun."

"So mote it be," intoned the pages.

Wyldon lowered his hands and the boys

dropped into their seats.

Kel, frowning, was less quick to sit. Had Lord Wyldon been talking about her? "Don't let his prayers bother you," Nealan told her, using his belt-knife to cut his meat. "My father says he's done nothing but whine about changes in Tortall since the king and queen were married. Eat. It's getting cold."

Kel took a few bites. After a minute she asked, "Nealan?"

He put down his fork. "It's Neal. My least favorite aunt calls me Nealan."

"How did his lordship get those scars?" she inquired. "And why is his arm in a sling?"

Neal raised his brows. "Didn't you know?"

If I knew, I wouldn't ask, Kel thought irritably, but she kept her face blank.

Neal glanced at her, shook his head, and continued, "In the war, a party of centaurs and hurroks—"

"Hur—what?" asked Kel, interrupting him.

"Hurroks. Winged horses, claws, fangs, very nasty. They attacked the royal nursery. The Stump—"

"The what?" Kel asked, interrupting again. She felt as if he were speaking a language she only half understood.

Neal sighed. There was a wicked gleam in his green eyes. "I call him the Stump, because he's so stiff."

He might be right, but he wasn't very respectful, thought Kel. She wouldn't say so, however.

She wasn't exactly sure, but probably it would be just as disrespectful to scold her sponsor, particularly one who was five years older than she was.

"Anyway, Lord Wyldon fought off the hurroks and centaurs all by himself. He saved Prince Liam, Prince Jasson, and Princess Lianne. In the fight, the hurroks raked him. My father managed to save the arm, but Wyldon's going to have pain from it all his life."

"He's a hero, then," breathed Kel, looking at Wyldon with new respect.

"Oh, he's as brave as brave can be," Neal reassured her. "That doesn't mean he isn't a stump." He fell silent and Kel concentrated on her supper. Abruptly Neal said, "You aren't what was expected."

"How so?" She cut up her meat.

"Oh, well, you're big for a girl. I have a ten-year-old sister who's a hand-width shorter. And you seem rather quiet. I guess I thought the girl who would follow in Lady Alanna's footsteps would be more like her."

Kel shrugged. "Will I get to meet the Lioness?" She tried not to show that she would do anything to meet her hero.

Neal ran his fork around the edge of his plate, not meeting Kel's eyes. "She isn't often at court. Either she's in the field, dealing with lawbreakers or immortals, or she's home with her family." A bell chimed. The pages rose to carry their empty trays to a long window at the back of the room, turning them over to kitchen help. "Come on. Let's get rid of this stuff, and I'll start showing you around."

Salma found them as they were leaving the mess hall. She drew Kel aside and gave her two keys. One was brass, the other iron. "I'm the only one with copies of these," Salma told her quietly. "Even the cleaning staff will need me to let them in. Both keys are special. To open your door, put the brass one in the lock, turn it left, and whisper your name. When you leave, turn the key left again. The iron key is for the bottom set of shutters. It works the same as the door key. Lock the shutters every time you leave, or the boys will break in that way. Leave the small upper shutters open for ventilation. Only a monkey could climb through those. Don't worry if any of the boys can pick locks. Anyone who tries will be sprayed in skunk-stink. That should make them reconsider."

Kel smiled. "Thank you, Salma."

The woman nodded to her and Neal, and left them.

Neal walked over to Kel. "If they can't wreck your room, they'll find other things to do," he murmured. When Kel raised her eyebrows at him, he explained, "I learned to read lips. The masters at the university were always whispering about something."

Kel tucked the keys into her belt-purse. "I'll deal with the other things as they come," she said firmly. "Now, where to?"

"I bet you'd enjoy the portrait gallery. If you're showing visitors around, it's one of the places they like to go."

After leading Kel past a bewildering assortment of salons, libraries, and official chambers, Neal showed her the gallery. He seemed to know a story about every person whose portrait was displayed there. Kel was fascinated by his knowledge of Tortall's monarchs and their families; he made it sound as if he'd known them all personally, even the most ancient. She stared longest at the faces of King Jonathan and Queen Thayet. She could see why the queen was called the most beautiful woman in Tortall, but even in a painting there was more to her than looks. The girl saw humor at the back of those level hazel eyes and determination in the strong nose and perfectly shaped mouth.

"She's splendid," Kel breathed.

"She is, but don't say that around the Stump," advised Neal. "He thinks she's ruined the country, with her K'miri notion that women can fight and her opening schools so everyone can learn their letters. Anything new gives my lord of Cavall a nosebleed."

"Still determined to go to war with the training master, Nealan?" inquired a soft, whispery voice behind Kel.

She whirled, startled, and found she was staring at an expanse of pearl-gray material, as nubbly as if it were a mass of tiny beads melted together. She stumbled back one step and then another. The pearl-gray expanse turned dark gray at the edges. Looking down, Kel saw long, slender legs ending in lengthy digits, each tipped with a silver claw.

She backed up yet another step and tilted her head most of the way back. The creature was fully seven feet tall, not counting the long tail it used to balance itself, and it was viewing her with fascination. Its large gray slit-pupiled eyes regarded her over a short, lipless muzzle.

Kel's jaw dropped.

"You're staring, Mindelan," Neal said dryly.

"As am I," the creature remarked in that ghostly voice. "Will you introduce us?"

"Tkaa, this is Keladry of Mindelan," said Neal. "Kel, Tkaa is a basilisk. He's also one of our instructors in the ways of the immortals."

Kel had seen immortals other than the spidren on the riverbank, but she had never been this close to one. And it—he?—was to be one of her teachers?

"We basilisks are travelers and gossips," Tkaa remarked, as if he had read her mind. "I earn my keep here by educating those who desire a more precise knowledge of those immortals who have chosen to settle in the human realms."

"Yes, sir," Kel said, breathless. She started to curtsy, remembered that a page bowed, and tried to do both. Neal braced her before she could topple over. Once she had regained her balance, the red-faced Kel bowed properly.

"I am pleased to meet you, Keladry of Mindelan," the basilisk told her as if he hadn't noticed her clumsiness. "I shall see you both the day after tomorrow." With a nod to Kel and to Neal, he walked out of the gallery, tail daintily raised.

Neal sighed. "We'd better get back to our rooms. Tomorrow's a busy day." He led her back to her room, pointing out his own as they passed it. "We'll meet in the mess hall in the morning," he told her.

Kel used the key as Salma had directed, and entered her room. Everything was in place, her bed freshly made up, curtains and draperies rehung. A faint scent of paint still drifted from the walls. "Gods of fire and ice, bless my new home," she whispered in Yamani. "Keep my will burning as hot as the heart of the volcano, and as hard and implacable as a glacier."

A wave of homesickness suddenly caught her. She wished she could hear her mother's low, soothing voice or listen to her father read from one of his books.

Emotion is weakness, Kel told herself, quoting her Yamani teachers. I must be as serene as a lake on a calm day. It was hard to control her feelings when so much was at stake and she was so far from home.

But control her feelings she would. If anyone here thought to run her off, they would find she was tougher than they expected. She was here to stay.

To prove it, she carefully unpacked each porcelain lucky cat and set it on her mantelpiece.

Only when she had placed each of them just so did she scrub her face and put on her nightgown.

Climbing into bed, she took a deep breath and closed her eyes. She imagined a lake, its surface as smooth as glass. This is my heart, she thought. This is what I will strive to be.

⊰ three ⊱

THE PRACTICE COURTS

*T*he next morning Kel heard the chatter of birds. She crept over to her open window and peered outside. It was nearly dawn, with the barest touch of light coloring the sky. Before her was a small courtyard with a single bedraggled tree growing at its center. On it perched house sparrows, drab in their russet brown and tan feathers, the males with stern black collars. Several birds pecked at the circle of earth around the tree. Kel watched them as the pearly air brightened. Poor things, she thought, they're hungry.

In her clothespress she had stowed the last of the fruitbread Mindelan's cook had given her for the journey south. Kel retrieved it and broke it up into crumbs, then dumped it on the courtyard stones. She was watching the sparrows devour it when the first bell rang and someone rapped on her door. She opened it and said a cheerful good morning to the servant who stood there with a pitcher of hot water.

"Good is as good does, Page Keladry," he said, his long face glum. He placed his burden on her desk. "I'm Gower. I'm to look after you." He began to sweep out the hearth as Kel took the water into her dressing room.

A new fire was laid when she returned to the main room, her face washed and her teeth clean. "If you've anything special you require, soap or cloths or such, tell me," Gower said sorrowfully. "Within reason, of course."

Kel blinked at him. She'd never met anyone this gloomy. "Thank you, Gower," she replied, intimidated. "I don't need anything just yet."

"Very good, miss," he said, then shook his head. "I mean, Page Keladry."

She sighed with relief when he left, and hurried to dress.

Undiscouraged by Gower, she wished Neal a good morning when she found him in the mess hall. He looked at her through bleary eyes and mumbled, "There's nothing good about it." Kel shook her head and ate breakfast in silence.

The day flew by. It began underground, where the palace stores were kept. A tailor took Kel's measurements. Then his assistant dumped a load of garments into her arms. She got three sets of practice clothes, sturdy tan cotton and wool garments to be worn during the morning. She also received three changes of the pages' formal uniform—red shirt and hose, gold tunic—to be worn in the afternoon and at royal gatherings. Shoes to match her formal gear were added; her family had supplied boots for riding and combat practice. Neal took the cloaks and coats she was given for cold weather.

Once she had stowed her things, Neal took her for another tour. They spent the morning inside, visiting the classrooms, libraries, indoor practice courts, and supply rooms like the pages' armory on the first level underground. After lunch, Neal took her to the outdoor practice courts and stables; the gardens, where she might wait on guests; and last of all, the royal menagerie. That night she dreamed the hooting calls of the howler monkeys from the Copper Isles and the chittering of brightly colored finches.

The next day she woke not to the gaudy finches' calls or the songs of Yamani birds, but to the friendly gossip of the courtyard sparrows. In hopes of seeing them again, she'd swiped a couple of rolls from the mess hall. Now she tore the rolls up and put the scraps outside the window for the birds.

As she finished, the bell rang. Gower rapped on her door as he'd done the day before, bringing hot water. Once he had cleaned the hearth and gone, Kel got dressed and ran to the mess hall. Her first day as a page had begun.

After breakfast, the pages flocked to one of the practice yards. Kel would take her first steps on the path to knighthood in these wood-fenced bare-earth rectangles and their adjoining equipment sheds. I'll work hard, she promised herself. I'll show everyone what girls can do.

Two Shang warriors, masters of unarmed combat, awaited the pages in the first yard. One of them sat on the fence, looking them over with pale, intelligent eyes. Her short-cropped tight gray curls framed a face that was dainty but weathered. She was clothed in undyed breeches and a draped, baggy jacket.

The other Shang warrior stood at the center of the yard, his big hands braced on his hips. He was a tall Yamani, golden-skinned, with plump lips and a small nose. His black eyes were lively, particularly for a Yamani. His black hair was cropped short on the sides and longer on top. His shoulders were heavy under his undyed jacket. Both he and the woman wore soft, flexible cloth shoes.

"For those who are new," he said, no trace of accent in his clear, mellow voice, "I am Hakuin Seastone, the Shang Horse. My colleague, who joined me this summer, is Eda Bell, the Shang Wildcat."

"Don't go thinking you can bounce me all over the ground just because I look like somebody's grandmother," the woman said dryly. "Some grandchildren need more raising than others, and I supply it." She grinned, showing very white teeth.

Kel saw the redheaded Merric swallow. She agreed: the Wildcat looked tough.

"You older lads, pair up and go through the first drill," ordered Hakuin. "Grandmother here will keep an eye on you. As for you new ones…" He beckoned them over to a corner of the yard. Once they stood before him, the man continued, "Your first and most important lesson is, learn how to fall. Slap the ground as you hit, and roll. Like this." He fell forward, using his arms to break his fall. The boys jumped; the sound and the puff of dust he raised made the fall appear more serious than it was.

The Horse got to his feet and held a hand out to blond Quinden. When the boy took it, he found himself soaring gently over Hakuin's hip. Only after he landed did the boy remember to slap the ground.

"You have to do that earlier, as you hit," said Hakuin gently, helping Quinden up. "Now." He beckoned to Kel and offered a hand.

She took it, meaning to let him throw her as he had Quinden, but the moment she felt his tug, six years of Yamani training took over. She turned, letting her back slide into the curve of his pulling arm as she gripped him with both hands and drew him over her right hip. He faltered, then steadied, and swept Kel's feet from under her. She released his arm, then tucked and rolled forward as she hit the ground. She surged back up again and turned to face him, setting herself for the next attack.

He stood where she had left him, smiling wryly. Horrified, Kel laid her hands flat on her thighs and bowed. She expected a swat on the head or a bellow in her ear—Nariko, the emperor's training master, had had no patience with people who didn't complete a throw or counter a sweeping foot.

When no one swatted or bellowed, she looked up through her bangs. Everyone was staring at her.

Kel looked down again, wishing she could disappear.

"See what happens when you get too comfortable, Hakuin?" drawled the Wildcat. "Someone hands you a surprise. If you'd been a hair slower, she'd've tossed you."

"Isn't it bad enough I am humbled, without you adding your copper to the sum, Eda?" the Horse inquired. "Look at me, youngster," he ordered. When Kel obeyed, she saw Hakuin's black eyes were dancing. "Someone has studied in the Yamani Islands."

"Yes, sir," she whispered.

"Your teacher was old Nariko, the emperor's training master, am I right? She always did like that throw. She drilled me in it so many times I wanted to toss her into a tree and leave her there."

Kel nodded, hiding a smile.

Hakuin looked at the older pages. "I believe you were practicing the first drill for the Wildcat?" he asked mildly. Instantly there was a flurry of activity, patterns of kicks, throws, and punches. Hakuin turned back to Kel. "Come show the other new ones how to fall. While they practice, we can see what else you know."

"Just what they taught the court ladies," Kel said. "Mostly counters to being grabbed or struck."

"You were with the embassy?" he asked.

Kel nodded.

"That explains everything." To the other new pages he said, "Watch how Keladry falls."

They all stared at her with a combination of confusion and dislike. It occurred to her that she had done the very thing her brother had warned her against. The other pages thought she was showing off. She couldn't help that now. The damage was done. She would just have to make sure that she didn't repeat her mistake.

With a sigh, she toppled forward, as she had so often in the islands, and smacked the ground.

When the next bell of the morning rang, they moved to another practice yard. A short black man in the maroon and beige uniform of the palace guard waited for them beside a barrel filled with long wooden staffs. Each of the pages selected one as he passed by.

"I am Sergeant Obafem Ezeko," announced the uniformed black man in unaccented Common. "Formerly weapons instructor to the Imperial Guard of Carthak, now serving the crown of Tortall. Lord Wyldon and I will instruct you in the use of various weapons. Pair up. You new ones at this end of the line. Cleon of Kennan and Vinson of Genlith, come up here to demonstrate."

Cleon was the big, redheaded boy who was Esmond of Nicoline's sponsor. He went to stand beside the sergeant, spinning his staff idly in his hands. Vinson faced off with him. He was a bony, tall youth. Kel had seen him eating with the handsome Joren at supper and breakfast.

"Show them a high block," instructed the sergeant. "Vinson defending, Cleon striking."

Cleon pulled his staff back and swung it first up, then down. The blow he'd aimed would have struck Vinson on the head or collarbone if it had landed. Instead Vinson gripped his staff, his hands spread wide apart, and raised the weapon a few inches over his head. Cleon's staff met his with a loud clack.

"Observe the strike," the sergeant told them. "Again, Cleon." The big youth repeated the strike, moving slowly. Kel nodded, watching the way his hands shifted on the smooth wood as he lowered it to tap Vinson's skull. From the way Vinson scowled at the bigger youth, Cleon's tap was a little harder than necessary.

"Your turn," barked Ezeko. He watched as the assembled pages did the strike. The newest boys were clumsy, although they should have had staff practice from their family men-at-arms. Kel was comfortable with the move. The only difference between this and the strike of a Yamani glaive, the weapon she knew best, was that she had no razor-sharp eighteen inches of steel at the end of her staff.

"Repeat the high block, Vinson," ordered the sergeant. Everyone watched as Vinson moved his hands apart on the staff and thrust it hard into the air, stopping just three inches over his head. He angled the staff down on the right to shield his face as well as his head. The sergeant made everyone do the same movement. He then had Cleon and Vinson demonstrate the middle strike and block, which centered on the chest and belly, and the low combination, to attack and defend the legs. Each time he made the pages try the moves.

Once they had practiced each movement, Ezeko had them stand in two lines. The newest pages were paired together. Neal, who was still new despite having been there during the spring and early summer, was partnered with Seaver of Tasride, the dark-haired, dark-eyed boy who looked as if he had a Bazhir ancestor. Kel was paired with redheaded Merric of Hollyrose. He was short, compact, and intent on their exercise. Kel licked her lips and settled the weapon in her hands.

"Left line strikes; right line blocks," the sergeant told them. He walked along the double line of pages, checking everyone's hold on the staffs. After he'd changed some boys' grips and nodded approval for others, he stepped back. "To my count," he bellowed. "High! Middle! Low!" Staffs clacked as the exercise began and wood met wood. "High! Middle! Low!"

Kel struck carefully. Proving herself tough on a smaller opponent wasn't right, and Merric looked nervous. The lightness of the staff bothered her. A Yamani glaive was far heavier. She knew that if she forgot she held a lighter pole, she would hit too hard.

"Faster! Swing 'em!" cried the sergeant. "I want to hear wood clack! You don't master the staff, you'll never master the sword. High! Middle! Low!" Over and over he chanted, increasing the speed. Kel bit her lip, locking her attention on the weapon.

"Ow!" someone cried as wood struck flesh. A few moments later there was another yelp.

"Keep going!" yelled Ezeko. "If your fingers hadn't been in the way, they wouldn't have gotten hit. Move 'em apart! The rest of you don't need me to count, do you? High, middle, low! I want to hear those staffs beat as one, understand me?"

They had been at it long enough to begin to sweat when Lord Wyldon came into the yard. He and Ezeko walked up and down the two lines of pages. Wyldon changed Prince Roald's footing. Ezeko corrected Esmond of Nicoline's grip. Wyldon thrust Neal's high block higher. They reviewed and changed each boy's work until they got to Kel and Merric. Rather than speak to them or change the way they exchanged blocks and strikes, both men turned and went back up the line, inspecting and correcting the other boys a second time. Kel watched them go; Merric banged her fingers as a result. When she looked at him, he glared at her.

It wasn't *my* fault they ignored us, she wanted to protest. She didn't. Warriors didn't make excuses.

"Switch places!" cried Ezeko when he reached the far end of the line of pages. They all stopped and repositioned themselves. Ezeko began the chant again. "High! Middle! Low!"

Merric seemed glad to be the one to hit. His blows fell harder and faster than the count, forcing Kel to respond in kind. Their rhythm fell out of time with their classmates'. Kel knew the men saw it, but they continued to focus their attention on the other pages. She kept up with Merric, blocking his strikes easily. She'd already attracted enough attention for one morning.

"Enough," said Lord Wyldon at last.

"Next," the sergeant informed them, "you will use strikes and blocks in combination. This time, strike your partner, then block his return strike."

"Change partners," added Wyldon. "Older pages, pair with the new ones, and see if you can better their speed. Come on, switch pairs!"

The boys looked around, trying to get to the partners they wanted before someone else did. Unsure of what to do, Kel remained where she was. When everyone formed into two lines once again, she was facing the beautiful Joren. Seeing that Kel stared at him, Joren smiled.

Kel hid her confusion. The day before, Neal had told her that Joren thought girls did not belong there. Now Joren smiled at her as if she were his friend. Does he want to make amends? she wondered.

"Get to it," Ezeko ordered. "Right line starts with a high strike. Left line does a high block, then a high strike. Right line, high block, then high strike. Older lads, go slow with the new ones. Strike! Block! Strike! Block! Nealan, stop flinching—if you get hit, you get hit. Strike! Block! Strike! Block!" He kept them at that for a few moments. Joren politely tapped his staff on Kel's as she blocked him; Kel then returned the hit and was blocked by Joren. They continued the rhythm easily.

"Switch to middle strike, middle block on my mark," Wyldon ordered. "Ready...middle strike! Middle block! Strike—King's Reach, stand still! You don't get dancing lessons till later."

Ezeko picked up the count. After a while they switched to putting low strikes against low blocks.

Kel relaxed. Joren was a good partner, meeting her with just the right amount of force. They traded blows and blocks easily, which gave Kel time to study him. Joren had to be the prettiest boy she'd ever seen. For all that he was older, a third-year page, he was only an inch taller, his gorgeous blue eyes nearly level with hers. He'd combed back his long, white-blond hair and secured it in a horsetail for the morning's work. If he were a player, Kel thought, they'd have him doing the young god Balcus Starsworn all the time.

Suddenly Joren's staff shifted under hers, sliding out of position for a block. He drove the lower end of his weapon under her guard, aiming for her ribs. Kel foiled him by stepping out of line.

"Back in place, probationer," barked Wyldon.

The exercise changed again, this time to a high strike against a high block, then a middle strike and middle block, followed by a low strike and low block. The speed picked up as well. More and more pages, not all first-years, began to make mistakes.

Ezeko stood by her and Joren, yelling out the

count. Kel took up the rhythm of the exercise, but now all of her senses were alert. When the pair next to them lost track of which block followed which strike, the sergeant moved to them. In the next moment Kel struck low and felt Joren's staff glide out from under hers. He swung his staff around and up, slamming it down at her collarbone. She whipped the foot of her staff up and around her arm to deflect him.

"This isn't a game, probationer!" snapped Wyldon. "Stick to the drill!"

Kel saw a mocking gleam in Joren's eyes. So Neal was right, she thought. He isn't nice at all.

Joren held to the drill, but now each block had more force behind it, making it a block and a blow. Each time he struck he was a little closer to her. Will they yell at him if he drives me back? Kel wondered. Or will they only yell if I move out of line?

"Come on, Queenscove!" cried Zahir, the tall young Bazhir page. "Stop flinching!"

Kel glanced over: Zahir was driving Neal out of the line of boys, his staff a blur in the air. Neal was blocking Zahir's strikes, but just barely.

Wyldon and Ezeko went to Neal and Zahir just as the tip of Joren's staff banged into Kel's cheekbone. He forced her backward, striking hard. She kept her fingers away from his weapon, thinking fast. If Wyldon or the sergeant wasn't going to put a stop to this, she had to.

She turned to the side, forcing Joren to move out of line to keep up. In turning, she discovered that the other boys had gathered around Zahir and Neal. They formed a kind of wall in front of Joren and Kel. Neither of the teachers would be able to see what Joren was doing until they forced the pages to form lines again.

Joren hit Kel hard and fast, raining blows on her. "Do you like this?" he demanded breathlessly as he pressed her. "Do you think you can keep up? Why don't you go home?"

"I belong here," Kel said grimly. She gave way before him, pushing his strikes to either side, thrusting their power away from her. "Just like the Lioness."

"Your precious Lioness is a mage and a cheat," sneered Joren, hate making him ugly. He tried thrusting his staff past her blocks. When she intercepted him, he'd swing to the side hoping to smash her ribs. Kel saw they had almost reached the barn that served as one wall of the yard. She would have to do something when they got there.

The butt of Joren's staff caught the big muscle in her left thigh. Kel winced, thinking that she'd had just about enough. Joren was all right with a staff, but he wasn't one of the emperor's ladies. Her brother had warned her against showing off her Yamani skills, but surely he didn't mean for her to lie down for a bully.

"Why don't you just get out while you can still walk?" Joren whispered as Kel ran into the barn. He faked a strike at her knee. When she blocked it, he turned his staff over, driving it at her ribs. This time Kel swung her weapon across her chest, pushing Joren's staff into the clear air at her side. Joren recovered, slightly off balance, and swung the butt of his weapon toward her ribs again.

Kel pivoted to the side, letting Joren's momentum carry him toward the barn. Holding her staff near the top, she thrust its low end between Joren's calves. He crashed face-first into the building. He spun—he was quick, she admitted—and struck at her wildly.

I'm done being polite, she thought grimly.

This time she thrust her staff under Joren's and up, between his hands. A quick twisting jerk yanked the wood from his grip and sent it flying. Kel then drove her staff toward the flesh at the base of his neck. There she let it rest. As Joren slid away from her along the barn, she followed, keeping the light pressure on his windpipe. If she'd had a glaive rather than a staff, she might have given him a scratch to make sure that he remembered the lesson.

"What on *earth* are you doing?" she heard Wyldon snap. "That was not staff work as it is practiced here!" Joren looked at him over Kel's shoulder. Kel kept her eyes on Joren, not trusting him.

"She trained in the palace of the Yamani emperor." The dry voice belonged to Eda Bell, the Shang Wildcat. "They're taught the use of a long-bladed pike—a glaive—there. How old were you when you started, Keladry?"

"Six," Kel replied. She finally lowered her staff and faced Wyldon.

The training master was red with anger. "This is Tortall, not the Yamani Islands—you are a noble, not a savage with a pigsticker. You will follow the assigned drills, understand? No Yamani cartwheels, no sleight of hand."

"It might be wise to teach Yamani methods," said Hakuin, the Shang Horse. Both he and the Wildcat leaned against the fence. Wyldon's claim that Yamanis were savages hadn't changed Hakuin's cheery look. He added, "You are friends with the Islands now, but that hasn't always been so. Even with a royal marriage arranged, there are always misunderstandings."

"I will take your words under advisement," Wyldon said tersely. "If we may now resume practice? With no more displays?"

But a pole arm makes it possible for a smaller warrior to take a big one, thought Kel, surprised by his attitude. That's why the imperial ladies are taught it, to save their honor and that of their charges.

"You practice with the probationer, Nealan," ordered Ezeko. "All of you, back in position!"

After more time spent on staff work, in pairs and alone, Wyldon and the pages ran down the long slope behind the palace to the archery range. Kel stayed away from him. After her bout with Joren, it had seemed that every time she turned around, Wyldon was ordering her to adjust her grip on her staff, change her stance, get her blocks higher, strike lower. It wasn't right—he wasn't correcting the boys nearly as much as he did her—

but she vowed she wouldn't let him know she thought so. She would prove that she could take whatever he threw at her.

At the archery range, she promised herself that she would not let any of the things she had learned in the Islands affect her work here. She might have carried it off if she had been able to go at her own pace. She knew she was in trouble when the archery master told them that since they were expected to already know how to use a long-bow, he wanted them to pick up their speed. He was everywhere, urging the pages to be quick, quick!

Soon everyone knew that when Kel got flus-tered, she gripped her bow in the wrong spot, two-thirds of the way down. Rushed, she drew the string with her thumb, not her index and middle fingers. She forgot that she used a short bow, and pulled the string back so far that the arrow dropped away. She bit her tongue and said noth-ing of the differences between Yamani archery and Tortallan. It's not like I was any good with a Yamani bow, she told herself. After Wyldon's comments about foreigners, Kel let him think she made silly errors as she concentrated on correcting her draw and her handling of the arrow.

Stone, she told herself as she picked up a dropped arrow, hearing giggles. For a moment she was five again, listening to the Yamani children laugh and tease the clumsy foreign barbarian. They accepted me in the end, she told herself. These boys will, too.

"Riding!" called Wyldon when the bell sounded the end of the class. "New boys, pick a mount from the spares. That horse will be yours to look after and ride for now. Saddle your mount and ride him out. Don't take forever!"

The pages set off for the stable at a trot. Halfway there, Kel noticed that the other four new pages were running full out to reach the stable first. She picked up her pace, knowing they wanted to beat her to the best choices of the spares. The group of older pages running ahead of her spread out and slowed down, blocking her without appearing to know she wanted to pass. When she got to the pages' stable, the new boys had made their selections. Their sponsors lounged in front of the stalls as if they dared Kel to even look at the others' selections.

They had left her two options. One was a chestnut mare with dull, uninterested eyes and a slumped stance. You could be after her a whole week before she'd take a step, thought Kel. The other horse was a small destrier, larger than most of the other mounts but not as big as the warhorses ridden by knights. A gelding, he was a strawberry roan: red-brown stockings, face, mane, and tail, and a white-flecked reddish coat. His attention was fixed on Kel, and there was a calculating look in his eyes. There were large scars on his legs and sides. White-haired spots on his back showed where he'd been saddled improperly in the past.

The other pages were halfway done saddling

their mounts. Neal worked on his horse, a neat brown mare, as he kept an eye on Kel.

Kel advanced to the dull-eyed mare, hand outstretched. She had to thrust it under the mare's nose before the horse would so much as sniff.

"She's the one you want," a man said, coming out of the shadows at the back of the stable. His clothes were spiked with hay and splashed with dried slobber; his blond hair looked as if horses grazed on it. Light blue eyes bulged slightly in his reddish face. The dull mare ambled over and nuzzled him. "She's a bit slow, but she's steady. Peachblossom there's ruined for knight's work—maybe ruined for work at all." He shook his head, eyes sad. "Dunno what I'll do with 'im if he won't take to cart or plow. They're after me to free up his box for when the new mounts come next week."

Kel could see it in the stableman's face: he did know what he would have to do. Horses cost money to keep. If they didn't pay for their stall and feed by working, unless they were good for stud they were put down.

She walked over to the gelding. Reaching into her pocket, she brought out the apple she'd put there and offered it to Peachblossom. The horse spent more time examining her than sniffing the treat, but he took the apple all the same.

"He won't bite, miss," said the hostler, coming over. "Not with me about. But I can't make him stay good, not without neglecting others. Sooner or later my effect on him will wear off. And he's got plenty of other tricks."

"I'll take—did you say Peachblossom?" she asked. "If he doesn't work out, I'll trade him for one of these new horses you're expecting."

"He's too big, miss," argued the hostler. "He's not for someone that's just learning how knights ride."

"Let me try, please," Kel replied. "I won't hurt him."

"It's not him I'm worried for," insisted the man.

"Have you made a choice, probationer?" demanded Wyldon. "We do ride today, remember."

The hostler grasped Peachblossom's head and laid his face on the horse's muzzle. "You'll be good, all right? I want you to, and sitting in here isn't what you're made for. Behave yourself, Peachblossom. You *do* know how." He released the horse and nodded to Kel. "He'll fare all right for a time, at least. If he gets shifty, tell him Stefan said 'be good.'" He ambled into the shadows at the stable's rear.

Kel found the gelding's tack and got to work saddling him. About to pull the girth tight, she found that Peachblossom was rounder than he'd first appeared. It was an old trick. The horse swallowed a bellyfull of air, making the saddle too loose, ensuring that the rider would slide off.

He's testing me, Kel thought. She kneed him in the belly. He turned and looked at her. "I'll tell Stefan on you," she whispered.

The horse blew out the air he'd sucked in. Kel cinched the girth tight. By the time Wyldon reached their end of the building, she and Peachblossom stood ready. Wyldon gazed at Kel and at the horse. If he thought the mount was too big and too hostile for Kel, he kept it to himself. Instead he ordered her to clean the tack well before she used it again. That done, he told the pages to lead their mounts outside and down the hill.

The practice yard was far enough from the stable that horses would not be forever trying to run for home. Kel was grateful for that. She was big for her age, but Peachblossom was big, too. If he raced for his stall she would flutter along behind him like a kite at the end of the rein.

Wyldon and the riding master stood beside the open gate to the yard and observed as each page walked his mount through. Once everyone was inside, the riding master ordered them to form a line, with the horses' heads facing inward. After inspecting the horses, the riding master said quietly, "Mount up."

Has anyone ever mounted *down*? Kel wondered as she swung into the saddle. The moment she settled, she thought that perhaps she'd been rash. Peachblossom's back was much wider than her pony's.

"Time was," Neal had explained the day before, "pages rode ponies till they were twelve or so. Our Stump, though, says that knights ride true horses, and so will pages. My father told me the number of broken bones from horse accidents has quadrupled since Wyldon became training master."

I should've taken the stupid one, thought Kel. This fellow is too much for me. Peachblossom sighed, as if he'd heard. Kel gritted her teeth. No. I'll keep him. He won't be pulling carts or killed for dogmeat, not while I have breath in my body. Knights ride horses, so pages ride horses, she told herself, and sat tall. Peachblossom looked back at her as if to say, Don't get cocky.

"Walk 'em sunwise," ordered the riding master. "A foot between you and the next rider."

Kel tugged the reins. Peachblossom didn't move. She tugged harder. Gods, his mouth must be as hard as stone, she thought, and yanked. At last the gelding understood, just as Wyldon ordered, "Move him along, probationer!"

Peachblossom turned and walked forward as soon as Kel nudged his sides with her feet. He paced along so amiably that Kel risked a look around. Most of the other mounts were restless, fighting rein and bit. Feeling better as she watched their riders struggle, she turned her eyes ahead. Peachblossom was stretching out his neck, trying to bite Neal's brown mare. Kel shortened her reins, pulling his head up. "You won't fool me," she whispered. The horse flicked an ear back toward her, listening. "I have nieces and nephews!"

Peachblossom blew out as if to say, Nieces and nephews are all very well, but they aren't *me*.

"Trot 'em," ordered the riding master.

Kel kept a watch on her mount. Peach-blossom obviously could not be left to his own devices for so much as a breath. The remainder of the lesson was a series of contests between her and the tricky gelding.

When Kel waddled out of the stable, her legs feeling as if she still had a mountain between them, Wyldon stopped her. "The boys use the men's baths," he said without meeting her eyes. "We made arrangements for your bathing, for all that I feel it is a mistake to make even a single exception for you."

So is this fair? Kel wondered. He's treating me differently from them. But I feel better about washing up by myself…It was too much to think about. She rubbed her head wearily. He seemed to want an answer of some kind. "I understand, my lord," she told him.

He lifted his eyebrows, as if he doubted she understood. "You will find a bath ready in your chambers," he said. "I expect you to be on time for lunch."

Kel bowed. "If I may go then, my lord?"

He nodded. She looked at the long, sloping rise to the palace. "You would do better to run that," remarked Wyldon. "You need the exercise. But I do not require it of the lads, and I will not ask it of you."

You won't ask it, but I'll do it anyway, she thought stubbornly. You'll see. I'm as good as any boy. I'm better.

Slowly, her legs protesting every step of the way, she began to trot up the hill.

⤦ four ⤧

CLASSROOMS

$\mathcal{A}$cademic classes began after lunch, just as Kel began to feel her bruises. Her first two classes—reading and writing, then mathematics—were taught by shaven-headed Mithran priests in bright orange robes. Not long after the pages' arrival, the teachers put them to work on their first written lessons of the year.

"History and the law of the realm," Neal murmured as they walked into their third class. "You'll like this!" He slapped a desk next to his. "Sit here. Sir Myles doesn't care where we put ourselves."

"Sir Myles?" she asked.

"Sir Myles, Baron of Olau, our teacher in history and law," Neal explained. "Why do you ask?"

Kel ran her finger over a scratch on her desktop. "He's the Lioness's father," she told him shyly. Seeing him would be almost as good as meeting Lady Alanna herself.

"Adoptive father, actually," Neal said as a small, chubby man entered the room. He was long-haired and bearded, dressed in a dark blue tunic over a dark gray linen shirt and gray hose.

His green-brown eyes were sharp as he looked over the pages.

"Here we are, trembling on the brink of a new year." Sir Myles ambled up to the front of the room and leaned against the wall. "I'm pleased to see no one swung his scythe too hard and cut off his own head—"

"But not for lack of trying!" joked the red-headed Cleon.

The knight raised gracefully curved brows. "You did not have to say that," he said mildly. "You would not be worthy to be a page if you were not always trying something." He perched on a tall stool. "Well," he said companionably, "we've had quite a year. Will someone explain why calling the recent deluge of battles the Immortals War is misleading? Your highness?"

Prince Roald ducked his head, but replied in a clear voice, "Because immortals—Stormwings, spidrens, ogres— were in the fight, but they were just allies to Scanrans, Copper Islanders, and Carthaki renegades. They weren't the leaders."

Sir Myles did not seem to care whether his students stood to answer. "Very good." The man looked around. "How many of your home fiefs took damage in the fighting?"

Hands went up, Kel's among them. No part of the realm was unscathed.

"How many know someone who was killed?"

Hands went up again. Kel knew of two people in the village who had been cut to pieces by killer centaurs. Luckily her own family had been spared the loss of any members.

"These losses are felt," Sir Myles told them. "Their majesties honor their sacrifice, and we all wish that it had not been needed." As the hands went down he said briskly, "Why did this happen? How did Scanra, the Copper Isles, and the Carthaki rebels come to assault our shores? Joren?"

The handsome boy lounged at his desk, seemingly bored. "The King's Champion killed a Copper Island princess thirteen years ago."

"That is one reason: bad blood. It doesn't explain the Carthakis and the Scanrans."

Joren shrugged. "Scanrans always raid us. They don't need a reason."

"But they do have reasons," Sir Myles pointed out. "Pressing ones that send them against us year after year. Put the Carthakis aside for now. Consider our gentle neighbors to the north. What riches do they have?"

"Furs?" suggested Faleron.

"Rocks," added Cleon, who got the laugh he'd intended.

The discussion went on. It ranged from poor Scanrans with failed crops to the destruction of the old Carthaki emperor and the installation of the new one, Kaddar. When the bell rang, it surprised Kel—she had lost all track of time.

"So what do you think of the king's spymaster?" Neal murmured in her ear as they left the classroom.

Kel came to a dead stop. "What?"

Neal smirked. "You didn't know. Myles of

Olau isn't just a teacher and a member of the King's Council. He's King Jonathan's spymaster."

"You're making that up," she accused him.

"Why?" he asked. "My father says he's the best spymaster the realm's had. It comes from Sir Myles going into trade to mend the Olau finances. His merchants send him all kinds of information—he just expands on it."

"Maybe you shouldn't tell," Kel pointed out. "Maybe it's supposed to be a secret."

Neal shrugged. "It's not talked of openly, but it's no secret. What's secret is who's his second in command, the one who does the legwork." He steered her into yet another classroom.

Kel came to a full stop again. All thought of spies and secrets evaporated from her mind. One entire wall of this classroom was filled with windows. Two walls were lined with shelves of glass containers, which enclosed plants, water, food dishes, even animals or fish.

Kel was glad to see that the other first-year pages seemed as amazed as she.

"Go ahead, look closer," Neal said. "Master Lindhall likes us to take an interest in the animals."

A small turtle was trying to bite Kel's index finger through glass when something white and clicky landed on her outstretched arm. It was a kind of living skeleton, a creature of bone and air. It had *flown* to perch on her, yet its wings were empty, slender fans made of very long finger bones. It gripped her arm with fossil claws. It tilted its long, pointed skull back and forth as if it were looking her over.

Leaning over, the thing clattered its jaws at her. Then it bit her nose so gently she felt only the barest pressure of its teeth.

"Bone!" A man strode over, brushing silvery blond hair from his eyes. "You must excuse Bonedancer," he told Kel in a soft and breathy voice. "There was no such thing as manners when he was alive, so he thinks he need not learn them now."

Bonedancer looked at him and clattered his jaws.

Kel looked at the skeleton, then at the man. He was nearly a foot taller than she, tanned and weathered, with broad cheeks and pale blue eyes. "I don't understand."

The man smiled. "A mage was briefly granted the power to raise the dead last year. Bonedancer was one of the things she brought back to life. He was a fossil then, and a fossil he remains. He's just rather more lively than most fossils."

It sounded like an explanation, but Kel was not sure she understood. I'll ask Neal, she told herself. "Thank you, sir," she told the man politely.

"I'm Lindhall Reed," he said to her and to the other first-years. "I am one of your teachers in the study of plants and animals. Have a seat, you new ones. As for everyone else, who has brought me a plant from home?" he asked. The older pages and Neal reached into their belt-purses to draw out leaves and stems wrapped in parchment.

Kel took a desk near the irritable turtle and waited for her head to stop spinning. She was positive that none of her brothers had mentioned flying skeletons when they talked about their studies.

After Master Reed's class, those who possessed a magical Gift went to study magecraft. Kel and the magic-less pages had a class with Tkaa the basilisk.

"For those who are new to the palace," the tall immortal began, "you should know that the king has decreed that those pages and squires without magic must learn to cope with magical things. You will have several teachers in this area. I will instruct you in the ways of immortals, of which I am one."

He bent down, until his large eyes gazed almost directly into Esmond of Nicoline's. "And immortals are…?" he inquired.

"Monsters?" replied the boy. He gasped, panicked. "I mean—I beg pardon! Not monsters, of course not." He fell silent as the basilisk laid a paw gently on his shoulder.

"Beings from the divine realms, who may live forever unless they are killed in some way," Seaver said quietly.

"Very good," replied Tkaa.

"Some *are* monsters, sir," added Seaver, meeting Tkaa's gaze steadily. "My father was killed by a spidren." Kel thought of the one that she had faced at Mindelan and swallowed hard.

"My sympathies," replied the basilisk with a

bow. "Spidrens *are* monstrous. Let me tell you of their creation, and of their habits."

The pages listened with fierce attention. Spidrens laired throughout the realm and were a deadly threat.

Their final class of the day was etiquette, taught by Upton Oakbridge, the royal master of ceremonies. The room was hot and the work so boring that Kel had to fight to stay awake. She ached all over from the morning's activity. The new pages were taught bows to nobles of different rank, which only made her muscles ache more. The older boys hid yawns as they practiced writing formal letters.

As the class drew to a close, everyone was given a book and assigned to report on its first chapter for the next day. When Kel saw the title, she grinned.

Oakbridge was on her like a cat. "What amuses you, probationary page?"

Can't he pretend I'm just like everyone else? thought Kel as she got to her feet. "Nothing, sir."

"But you are amused, it was quite clear. You must share the joke with us, probationary page, now, if you please." He stood before her desk, one fist planted solidly on a hip. She could hear his foot tapping briskly.

"Master Oakbridge—"

"Lord Wyldon shall school you properly in the matter of excuses. I will accept no more evasion, probationary page!"

Kel opened the book and pointed to the

author's name. "Sir, the writer is my father."

The master of ceremonies snatched the book away and scowled at the title page. "What of that?" he demanded. "The child does not have all of his father's knowledge."

All of *her* father's knowledge, thought Kel irritably.

"Excuse me, Master Oakbridge," Neal said in his friendliest voice, "but Kel doesn't have all of *her* father's knowledge. Not *his*."

Dropping her blank Yamani mask-face, Kel glared at him.

Oakbridge also glared at Neal. "The majority of you are lads. Proper usage calls for male pronouns when males are part of the group."

"Except that you addressed Kel alone, which then demands the exact term."

Kel clenched her hands behind her, where Master Oakbridge could not see them. She promised herself that from now on she would try to sit as close to Neal as possible. She could not kick someone eight chairs away.

Oakbridge gave Neal a look that would have stripped paint, then turned back to Kel. "You have not answered me," he said. "Have you your father's knowledge? You are but a child."

"Yamani etiquette is serious," Kel replied, her face once more Yamani-calm. "Especially at the emperor's court. People have their heads cut off if they don't bow right."

Oakbridge stared at her for a moment. Then he pursed his lips. "Review this entire volume tonight, probationary page Keladry," he announced. "Tomorrow you will report on those parts that are familiar to you, and which parts, if any, are not. Should I be satisfied as to the breadth and depth of your knowledge, I may call on you to assist me in preparing for courtesies to the Yamanis." To the pages he explained, "As I am certain his highness is well aware"—he looked at Prince Roald, who nodded—"their majesties have arranged for a state visit next fall by Princess Chisakami of the Yamani Empire. When she arrives, we shall know how to greet her and her attendants properly, according to their own custom. To that end—"

The final bell of the afternoon rang. Kel gathered all her papers and books and followed the other pages out of the room.

Neal was waiting. "So, probationary page…" He grinned as Kel made a face. "How long did you live with the Yamanis?" They headed back to their rooms.

"Six years," she replied. "Longer than I've lived in Tortall, actually."

"Can you speak—" Neal began as they stopped before Kel's door. He interrupted himself to sniff the air. "What's that smell?"

Kel leaned closer to her door and sniffed. "Urine," she said. There was a pool of yellowish liquid on the threshold. "I'd better clean it up."

"No," ordered Neal. "You have to change for supper. I'll tell Salma and meet you in the mess hall. Get moving." He trotted away, shaking his head.

Kel juggled her school materials until she could pull out her key, then opened the door. At least none of the urine had leaked into the room; that was a blessing.

She closed the door with a sigh. What a disappointing day! Parts of the morning's exercise had been interesting, but the classwork was simply tedious. What good would etiquette do a knight? And how could she be expected to stay awake all afternoon when she'd been running all morning? Couldn't she just do the physical training and forget learning a whole new set of bows?

It is not your place to question what the masters want you to learn, she told herself. Your place is to obey. It was what her Yamani teachers would have said if they had heard Kel's unhappy thoughts.

I just wish obedience was more exciting, she told them silently as she began to change her clothes for supper. Is that so much to ask?

Once they had filled their trays, Kel and Neal went to the spot they had claimed as their own and sat. Kel picked up her fork, but Neal shook his head. She looked around. All of the boys had taken their places, but no one had begun to eat. She raised her eyebrows at Neal, who whispered, "No Stump."

Everyone fidgeted; Kel's stomach growled. At last the door opened. The squires jumped to their feet and bowed. Someone murmured, "The king."

Then everyone was up and bowing as two

men—the king and Lord Wyldon—walked up to Wyldon's small table. Kel stared at the ruler whose domain she wanted to serve so much. King Jonathan was the handsomest man she had ever seen. He was an inch shorter than Wyldon, but the training master faded beside him. King Jonathan's neatly trimmed hair and beard were coal-black, framing a face that was tan from a summer outdoors. His nose was straight and proud. His eyes were a deep, brilliant sapphire blue, framed by long lashes. On any other man those lashes might have seemed feminine; not on the king.

He grinned; white teeth flashed against the black of his beard. "Don't let me keep you from your meal," he said in a clear baritone voice. "I remember what it was like from my own days at those tables."

"If your majesty will give the blessing?" asked Wyldon, half bowing.

The king nodded. He stepped up to the lectern, raising his hands. "Bright Mithros, Great Mother, all gods powerful and small, grant us your blessings and guidance, we humbly pray." He brought his hands together, and his audience realized he'd finished.

"So mote it be," responded the pages and squires raggedly. They had expected a longer prayer.

"Now eat," said the king. "After you're done, I'd like a word." He and the training master sat at Lord Wyldon's table. The fourth-year page whose task it was to wait on them rushed to put food before the two men.

Kel eased back onto her seat, her thoughts all in a jumble. She tried to sort them out as she ate. She wished she could ask the king why he had allowed Lord Wyldon to put her on probation for a year. In that original proclamation ten years ago, it was written that girls could try for their knight's shield; probation had not been mentioned. It wasn't fair, so why had he allowed it? Could she serve a king who wasn't just with her? Chivalry worked two ways: you gave good service to your overlord, and in return your overlord honored your service and treated you honestly. None of this adding extra conditions when all you wanted was the same chance everyone else got.

I suppose I'll never find the courage to ask him why flat out, she thought sadly. I'll just bow and be polite like a good ambassador's daughter. I bet Neal wouldn't hesitate to ask. She looked at her sponsor and smiled in spite of herself. Neal was eating his cake as his vegetables got cold on his plate.

When everyone had finished, the king went to stand at the lectern again. "Don't get up," he said as everyone began to rise. "If memory serves me, your legs are starting to get sore right about now."

A number of the boys chuckled. Kel looked at her hands, which were curled into fists in her lap. If you can't treat me properly, I'm not going to laugh at your jokes, she thought stubbornly.

"I won't keep you long," the king promised. "I really just wanted to look at you.

"We survived the Immortals War, as they're calling it. We survived, but at a price. You know as well as I how many knights were lost, how many crippled. Thanks to Lord Wyldon, you older pages and squires were also able to fight, to defend our people. You did well—but I can see there are faces gone from this room who were present last fall. We shall miss those who are gone.

"Our enemies tried to destroy us. They failed—but we are hurt. Inside these walls, I can tell you, we are hurt. Our healing will be the work of years."

No one spoke. No one moved.

"Most importantly," he continued, speaking as he might to his closest friends, "it is the work of *your* years. Your studies, your bruises, your saddle sores, your nights spent doing mathematics, and history, and mapmaking. Your mastery of the arts of war, and of the laws of the realm."

King Jonathan paused for a moment, his eyes exploring their faces. Looking at him, Kel thought grudgingly, All right, he hasn't been fair, and he hasn't made Lord Wyldon treat me like the boys, but he's right about the work. I'll show them—I'll show him, and Lord Wyldon—that I'm as good for that work as anybody else. Like the emperor's Chosen warriors. I'll be an example. They'll be sorry they ever treated me unjustly.

"Each one of you here is a gem, all the more precious because we lost so many. Combined, you are the treasure of the kingdom. Treat yourselves as such. Work hard, study hard, and know your value. Guard your strength, make it grow. Build your stores of learning. Do it not for yourselves or your teachers or your monarchs. Do it for the kingdom. Do it for us all." He looked them over one last time, nodded briskly, then strode out of the hall. He was gone before any of them remembered to bow.

As unhappy as her thoughts had been, Kel still had to remember to take a breath once the king had left the room. His presence was even stronger than the emperor's had been. She could see how people might fight and die for him, and how he could stir such fierce loyalty in calm and level-headed men like her own father. Just a look around the room showed her boys who were still caught up and breathless after what he'd said. Even Neal, who seemed so world-weary, looked eager.

When he realized her eyes were on him, he smiled. "Isn't this a great time to be alive?" he asked. "Stormwings and spidrens to fight, beings from legends arrayed at our sides, people in need of protection and us being prepared to do it…Nothing happened in King Roald's time, and everything's happening now. We'll be sung about, our names will be passed on to our descendants."

"It's going to take a lot of work, that's for certain," she replied with a shrug.

Neal propped his chin on one hand and gazed at her. "You aren't a bit romantic, are you?" he asked, amused.

She sat back and stared at him. She was beginning to think that Neal required a keeper. He seemed to have the craziest ideas. "Romance? Isn't that love-stuff?" she asked finally.

"It's more than just love. It's color, and—and fire. You don't want things magnificent and filled with—with grandeur," he said, trying to make her understand. "You know, drama. Importance. Transcendent passion."

"I just want to be a knight," Kel retorted, putting her used tableware on her tray. "Eat your vegetables. They're good for you."

When she returned to her room, Kel found a small package on her desk. She looked it over. It was wrapped in canvas and addressed to her. The writing was ornate yet readable, like the style that market scribes used. The twine and canvas both were cheap quality, available to anyone with a few coppers to spend.

She drew her belt-knife to cut the twine, sawing until the cord parted. Kel put the blade down with a sigh. She would have to sharpen it yet again. It got dull very quickly. She hadn't thought to ask her parents for a new one before she left home.

Opening the canvas wrap, she found a plain wooden box inside. Shaking her head—she didn't like mysteries of any kind—Kel opened the box. Inside she found a sheathed belt-knife. Like the box, the sheath was plain, made of the same kind of black leather that wrapped the hilt. The blade itself was a very different matter: it was steel as fine as anything that came out of the Yamani Islands, so sharp it would slice a hair. Kel knew that because the first thing she did was pluck one from her head and draw it lightly over the edge.

Underneath the knife was a small leather bag with a whetstone. Like the sheath and box, the bag was ordinary. The stone was high-quality goods. It would put on an edge even her old knife would hold.

Inside the bag was a parchment tag. Written on it, in that same common lettering, was "Goddess bless."

Kel had to sit on the bed. Who would send such a fine gift? Anyone in her family would include a proper note. Neal was friendly, but she couldn't see him spending this kind of money on her. She couldn't see anyone doing it.

She thought it over until the first after-supper bell rang: she had classwork, and Neal had invited her to study with him. Fretting over the identity of the gift-giver would not be of much use for now. She removed her old knife and clipped the new one to her belt, smoothing it with careful fingers before she gathered her books. The gift had come the first day of real classes, which told her there was one thing she could be sure of: someone wished her well.

Kel smiled. Someone wanted the probationary page to succeed.

⇥ five ⇤

KEL BACKS AWAY

*F*ive weeks after her arrival at the palace, Kel decided to write a letter to her family. It was hard to get started. That morning Peachblossom had stepped on her foot, bruising it even through her heavy riding boot. It seemed to hurt worse as the day wore on, distracting her in her classes and at supper. Only when she had propped the foot on a cushion placed on a stool did the throbbing ease enough to allow her to write.

Dear Papa and Mama,

Thank you for the package with the candied fruit and cakes. I shared with my sponsor, Nealan of Queenscove. He liked the cakes very much.

I can't believe that five whole weeks have gone. I am working hard. The teachers are strict. Master Oakbridge, the master of ceremonies, is teaching Yamani etiquette from Papa's book. I have to show everyone the submissions so much that I get dizzy. My favorite class is mathematics. I think the teacher, Master Ivor, is pleased with my work.

Tell Tilaine there are no banquets until

Midwinter Festival so I haven't served the king at table yet. Pages get to practice serving Lord Wyldon and his guests at supper three days in a row. The new pages are last on the schedule so my turn won't come until late this year. I won't get to serve at the high table at Midwinter. Only senior pages get to wait on important people like the king.

I have a horse. He is a strawberry roan gelding named Peachblossom. He is too big for me, but I like him. He will be sold or killed if I do not keep him. He is very clever, and plays all kinds of tricks if I do not keep an eye on him.

Also, might I have some green tea from our stores? It is <u>very</u> expensive here, and I truly need something to drink at night as I do my classwork.

I did not pack enough dresses. We are allowed to wear our own clothes to supper unless there is a feast or something. Might I have some of my other gowns and some more shifts? And could they be let down an inch? I have grown a little.

Kel smiled at the last paragraph, knowing it would surprise her mother. She had always preferred breeches for wear at home, unless they had to don kimonos for an event at the emperor's court. These days, however, Kel wore dresses whenever possible. She was not about to let the pages forget that there was a girl in their midst. Gowns at supper were just one way to remind them.

What else could she tell her family? Kel stared at her letter, drumming her fingers. She decided to leave out that sometimes Prince Roald sat with her and Neal at supper. For one thing, it seemed like bragging. After all, the prince had made it a point to sit at meals with each of the pages at least once during the weeks since her arrival. That he sat with her and Neal the most could simply be due to his curiosity about the Yamanis. Kel suspected that Prince Roald wanted no one to guess that he was fretting about his coming marriage to Princess Chisakami. Instead she wrote:

Does Mama still have her sketchbook from the Islands? Her pictures are better than the ones in books in the palace libraries. Neal wants to know what things look like.

That was true enough. Neal *was* curious about the Yamanis and how they lived, and if the prince also looked at the sketches, so much the better.

She would not mention the bad things that happened, not the boys' tricks or Peachblossom's bad habits. That seemed too much like whining to her. Instead she shifted her foot to a better spot on the cushion and wrote on:

There are sparrows who come to me for bread and the seed I get from the stables. They are practically tame, and eat at my windowsill. One of them is a female with a pale spot on her head. I named her Crown. She scolds the others and she is always the first at the food, so I think of her as their queen. The sparrows get up before dawn, and it is nice to hear them chirp while I dress. There is an amazing lizard-bird skeleton that is actually alive in my class on plants and animals. He likes bread too. Lucky for me, Neal said we can ask the cooks for extra food so I am not forever trying to sneak rolls out of the mess hall!

What else could she say? They didn't have to know that only Neal and the prince would talk to her, or that yesterday she had been doused in a bath of muddy water when she stepped out of her room. Thanks to that she had been *very* late to breakfast, causing the boys to growl as she came in. For her lateness, Wyldon had given her a week of mucking out the stables from the first bell after supper until the second bell. She would just finish her letter with the cheerful bit about the sparrows.

Once she had finished, she turned to get her sealing wax and seal from her desk drawer. Her bruised foot slipped from its pillow to bang on the floor. She yelped.

Someone knocked on her door. "Kel, open up. It's me, Neal."

"Drat," she muttered, and went to let him in.

As he stepped into the room, he saw her lucky cats. "Why are those things waving?"

She smiled. "The legend is that a cat waving to the first emperor drew him out of the path of an enemy arrow. The Yamanis make hundreds of them. They're supposed to bring luck."

"Good thing you have so many, then," remarked Neal, picking one up and examining it.

Kel made a face at him. "Very funny." She hobbled over and put the cat back where it belonged.

"I *thought* you were limping in the mess," he said. "Have a seat and let me take a look."

"The door stays open," she warned him.

"Yes, yes, yes. Why are you holed up in here?" he demanded. "Come study with Roald and me."

"I will," she said, wincing as she lowered herself onto her bed. "I just had to finish a letter home. I wanted to thank them for the cakes and things."

Neal grabbed her footstool and sat by the bed. Gently he lifted her swollen foot onto his knees. "And you say Peachblossom wasn't trying to hurt you?" he said. Her foot was one large bruise.

"He wasn't," Kel retorted. "If he'd been *trying*, he'd have broken it. I really think he's starting to like—ow!"

"There's no reason why you should have this kind of pain," muttered Neal, inspecting her toes. "It figures. You aren't at all ticklish."

"Very funny," she retorted, eying him nervously. "What are you going to do?"

"Fix it," he said. "Foot bruises take forever to heal without help."

"I don't know," Kel protested, carefully drawing her foot away. "The Yamanis say it's better to live with pain. You have to let it roll away like water off a stone. That way it doesn't have any power over you."

"They sound like wonderful, cheerful people,"

commented Neal. "Any other useful warrior stoic arguments?"

Kel shook her head. "What would Lord Wyldon say if he knew? He told us knights work through pain all the time. He does it himself, you can see it hurts him to use that arm." Wyldon had shed his sling a week after the start of classes, and used his right arm now in weapons practice and riding. "Sometimes there's no healer around, or others need a healer more than you."

"Well, you're neither a stone nor a Yamani nor the Stump, in case you haven't noticed," Neal said tartly. "And it's foolish to stint on healing in a palace full of mages. Don't argue anymore." His voice was firm but his hands gentle as he drew her leg back onto his knees.

Kel thought of her Yamani teachers, who were taught as children to sit unmoving in icy rains for as much as an entire day. She *was* being weak, letting Neal do this. She ought to refuse the help, but she couldn't. Her foot hurt too much.

Neal rested her foot on his hands and bowed his head. A soft light of such a deep green as to be nearly black shimmered between his palms and Kel's flesh. She felt it as coolness that sank under her skin, and sighed. The pounding in her foot began to soften until it had ceased. Her toes shrank back to their normal size as she watched.

"I can't believe you gave up learning to be a healer," Kel said when Neal released her foot. "I can't believe you're happier as a page. An *old* page, at that!"

Neal made a face. "I can name three who were older when they started."

"Please don't," Kel said hurriedly. Once Neal started to give lists of things, even a three-person list, he would not be content until he also mentioned what books he'd learned their names from, who wrote them, and who disagreed with the writers of the original books. It was far easier not to let him get started. She said, "And don't tell me you did all this to be one of the oldest first-year pages in the realm."

Neal sighed, surveying his long-fingered hands. "On the Great Roll of Knights in the Hall of Crowns, twelve Queenscove knights are listed—only the Naxens have more. In *The Scroll of Salute*, King Jonathan the First wrote that four houses were the shield of Tortall: Legann, Naxen, ha Minch, and Queenscove. My brothers thought knighthood was the greatest service they could give."

"But it isn't the only service *you* can give," protested Kel. "You've got brains. You've got the magical Gift. Why are you bashing about here?"

"Keeping you out of trouble," Neal said cheerfully. "Try resting your weight on that." As Kel stood and walked under his gaze, he continued, "As to that ill-tempered nag of yours, I have an idea."

She was no scholar, but she knew when a subject was closed. "He's not a nag, and I won't take another horse."

"I *know* that," said Neal, exaggeratedly patient.

"But perhaps we can have someone talk to him on your behalf. Come on."

He led her at a brisk walk through the classroom floor to a broad stair, up two stories, and down a hall. "The academics' rooms are on this floor and the one below," he explained. "Some of our teachers—the ones who aren't priests—live here. You won't get these two until later this year in magic class."

Neal strode to a door decorated with a bronze nameplate. *Numair Salmalín* was engraved in the metal. Below it, in letters more recently added, was the name *Veralidaine Sarrasri*. He rapped hard, then waited, shifting his weight from foot to foot. Why is he nervous, all of a sudden? wondered Kel.

The door opened a crack and a young woman peered out. Brown curls tumbled around a face lit by blue-gray eyes. Her mouth was soft, her chin roundly stubborn. "Neal, hello," she whispered with a smile. "Did you want Numair? He's sleeping. He was up all last night and half today on a working."

"Actually, Daine, I wanted to ask a favor of you," Neal replied, keeping his own voice to a whisper. He was even more nervous than he'd been a moment ago. "It's for my friend Kel, here. And her horse."

He likes her, Kel realized with amusement. A *lot*. She'd had experience with crushes—none of her own, of course, but her older sisters Adalia and Oranie were very prone to them.

Daine walked into the hall, closing the door gently behind her. "A horse?"

"He's contrary and mean," explained Neal, "and Kel here won't give him up. Keladry of Mindelan, this is Veralidaine Sarrasri. Daine, Kel."

Kel bowed.

"You're the one Bonedancer likes," Daine told her with a nod. "Lindhall says he's taken to you. And Neal doesn't like your horse."

Kel shrugged. She hardly knew what to say. She'd heard so many odd stories about this woman since her family had returned from the Yamani Islands.

"We were thinking—I was thinking—you might take a look," explained Neal. "He's got a mouth like stone—can it be fixed? And he's mean clear through."

"Let me see him," Daine replied. "What's his name?" Her eyes focused on Kel's, as if she could see into the girl's heart.

"Peachblossom," Kel said.

It wasn't until Daine smiled that Kel could look away from those blue-gray eyes. "Peachblossom? Not one I know, but then, I have little to do with the nobles' horses," she explained. "Let's have a look at him."

Neal did the talking as they walked down to Peachblossom's stable. He asked Daine a great many questions about people Kel did not know. She followed them, feeling out of place.

When they entered the stable, all of the horses

came to the front of their stalls to greet Daine. Shyly Kel pointed her gelding out. Daine went to Peachblossom and stood nose to nose with him, her hands cupped under the horse's chin. Peachblossom's ears were pricked forward with interest. He was more relaxed with Daine than Kel had ever seen him.

Neal made the mistake of trying to stroke him. Back went the gelding's ears; up went his head. Neal snatched away his hand. "Excuse *me,*" he muttered.

Ignoring him, Daine ran her hands over the horse, inspecting every inch. Kel watched the examination. Peachblossom seemed to like Daine's touch. When she was finished, he rested his nose against her gown, which was now covered with horsehair.

"What do you want of him?" Daine asked Kel. "I can soften his mouth, but if you're forever dragging at the rein, it'll just get hard again. Stefan's done wonders with these scars, though Peachblossom says they still pain him some. I can mend those, but if you make him fight and you spur him as some do their mounts, he'll be scarred again. And I can't change his nature for you. Peachblossom is who he is; no one has the right to take that away."

"I wouldn't ask it," Kel replied firmly. "We get on all right." Neal snorted. Kel ignored him, telling Daine, "If he didn't hurt from his scars, that might help, and softening his mouth would be a blessing. I'm not one for using the rein hard."

"That's what he says. He also says that if you promise never to use spurs, he'll mind his manners a bit more."

"She has to have spurs when we get to riding in armor," Neal pointed out. "The St—Lord Wyldon makes all the third- and fourth-years wear them."

"There are spurs that don't cut the horse," said Daine quietly. "Peachblossom will settle for those. You really want to keep him?"

Kel shrugged. "It's drawing carts or death if I don't."

"I'll buy him," Daine offered. "I think I have enough. I'd take him off your hands and find you a better mount."

Peachblossom turned his head away from Daine to look at Kel. She felt a pang at the thought of losing him. She admired the big gelding's independence, the way he didn't seem to care if people liked him or not. She wished she could be more like that. Peachblossom would be happier with someone who could talk to him, though. Daine would be good to him.

Peachblossom put two hooves back, then two more. Another step, and he could turn away from Daine to face Kel. His ears twitched forward. When Kel, unbelieving, held out her open hand— as Neal winced—Peachblossom lowered his head and softly lipped her palm.

"That's that," remarked Daine. "He says you

need looking after."

"I never thought I'd end up agreeing with a horse," murmured Neal.

Peachblossom's ears went flat. He blew a wad of spit onto Neal's shirt.

"He also says because he will let Kel ride him doesn't mean he has to be nice to everyone," Daine remarked, her eyes twinkling. "Come to me, Peachblossom. We've still your hurts to mend." To Kel she added, "I'll teach him spoken commands for when you need him to go faster. You won't need spurs with those."

Neal walked Daine back to her rooms. Kel returned to the page's wing alone, feeling very much in the way and thinking of the classwork on her desk. On the way she stopped at the mess hall kitchen. She helped herself to an apple and begged two rolls for her sparrows from a cook.

She was near her room when voices drew her attention. They came from the hall ahead. "Pages are supposed to be graceful, not clumsy." Kel knew Joren's mocking tones well. She froze.

"Clumsy?" She also knew Merric's voice.

Something clattered and crashed; a boy yelped. Kel turned into the hall to see what was going on.

Three older pages stood over Merric, who had fallen. Apparently he'd been carrying a heavy pitcher and cups on a tray. Now milk had splashed everywhere and the dishes lay in pieces.

"Don't just grovel there," jeered Vinson, one of Joren's friends. "Stand and mop it up."

"Fetch us another pitcher of milk, and fresh cups," added Joren. "How can we study if we are thirsty?"

Kel clenched her fists. It was the custom that Anders had described, the one in which older pages made first-years do errands to earn their right to be considered true pages. Kel had done such errands herself for the prince. Most senior pages understood that first-years had little time for their work and gave them tasks that were small and quickly done. But she'd heard whispers that Joren liked the custom a bit too much, and liked to add a bit of pain to his errands.

Merric stood, dripping milk, his pale face crimson with shame. "I'll need cloths," he said.

Joren planted his hand on the smaller boy's back and shoved. Merric's feet slipped; he flew forward, landing on his face again. "Use what you're wearing for cloths," Joren said merrily. "They're doing well enough so far!"

"And shut up while you're at it," added Vinson.

The third member of their trio, Zahir, caught sight of Kel. He elbowed Joren and pointed to her.

"Get mopping," Joren ordered Merric. "Every drop, mind." He turned to Kel. "What's the matter with you, *probationer?*" he demanded coldly.

Kel clenched her fists. "This is servants' work," she said. "It has nothing to do with being a page and fetching and carrying for people. It isn't what's meant by earning our way."

Joren took a step forward. "This is none of your affair—unless you want what he's getting."

Merric looked at Kel, then away. Kel remained where she was, frozen with indecision. They were older, taller, and faster, with every muscle trained hard by Lord Wyldon. These student warriors would outrank her in the Yamani Islands. There she would owe them her obedience.

In Yaman, picking on a younger warrior would be considered a waste of the time owed to your overlord, she thought numbly.

If I interfere, I might give Lord Wyldon an excuse to get rid of me, she realized.

Joren's face went even harder. He came down the hall, fists raised.

For the first time in her life, Keladry of Mindelan ran from a fight with a bully. Reaching the safety of her room, she locked the door behind her. Even there, she thought she could still hear the laughter that had followed her escape.

Somehow she managed a little classwork before the bell rang for bed. She got into her nightdress and crawled under the covers, shivering. Over and over she saw the scene in her mind, with poor Merric outnumbered and unable to fight back. He'd been right to be afraid, she told herself repeatedly. *She'd* been right to be afraid. Giving way to superior force was how their world worked. Someday she and Merric both would show Joren and his crew how it felt to be humiliated and afraid.

Someday they would fear *her*.

So, if she thought they would fear her, why didn't she feel better? She'd done the wise thing. Hadn't she?

You could tell on them, a voice whispered in her heart. You know they tripped Merric deliberately. No one is supposed to take the earning-your-way custom that far.

She flinched at the thought. Pages were not tattletales. They dealt with problems or suffered in silence. Everyone would despise her for breaking that unwritten law. Wyldon would despise her. Her brothers would shake their heads in shame. She would be sent home.

You saw a bad thing done and you didn't raise a hand or speak out, argued her better self. Could you swear a knight's oath, knowing that you once let bullies get away with it?

If I get in fights, won't Lord Wyldon use that as an excuse to be rid of me?

Perhaps not. She'd heard Anders's stories. Pages were *expected* to fight, win or lose, and take the punishments doled out. Alanna the Lioness was in fights as a page. She got punished for them all. She took her punishment and never gave up the names of those she'd fought with. That was how things were done.

Of course none of them had been on probation. Only Keladry of Mindelan was served *that* bowl of sour soup.

Stop feeling sorry for yourself! she scolded,

trying to find a spot in her bed that wasn't hot from her thrashing around. We don't argue with custom; we obey it. Wiser people than us started such things, it's as simple as that.

But what if custom is wrong? demanded the part of her that believed in the code of chivalry. A knight must set things right.

I'm not a knight yet, she told herself, punching a pillow that seemed determined to smother her. I'm not even a real page. I'll worry about things like that when I am.

Shouldn't I worry about them all along? If I don't worry about them as a page or a squire, why should I care when I am a knight?

At last she slept.

The first thing she noticed that was not part of her unhappy night was the prickle of tiny claws on her hand. She opened her eyes and looked down. A sparrow—the female with the spot on her head that Kel had named Crown—stood on her hand, looking at her. Crown turned her head this way and that, as if trying to decide what to do with this great lazy girl who lay abed when the sun was about to rise.

Kel looked at her windows, certain she had not opened the lower set of shutters the night before. She was right. Only the small upper shutters were open. Crown had flown in through those, seeing well enough in the pre-dawn glow to land safely on Kel.

It seemed the bird had exhausted her supply of

patience. She jumped onto Kel's chin and pecked her gently on the nose.

"All right," Kel croaked. At the first movement of her chin, the bird hopped back to her chest. "Tell your friends I'm coming."

Crown flew up and out of the open shutters, for all the world as if she had understood.

Neal said the animals around here are strange, Kel thought, tossing her blankets aside. I guess he's right.

Lurching to the windows, she opened the lower shutters. The sparrow flock, brown and tan females and black-collared males alike, sat on the sill in a line, watching her.

"I hope you had a better night than I did," Kel told them, getting her rolls and seed.

In the mess hall, Neal squinted at her as she toyed with her breakfast. "You look as bad as I feel," he croaked. "Where's the sunny smile? The 'Hello, Neal, isn't it a *wonderful* day to be alive in the royal palace?' pain-in-the-bum greeting I usually get?"

Kel considered shoving her porridge into his face and decided against it. "I don't know," she said at last. "Why don't you go look for it?"

Neal sat up. "Ouch. It bites."

"What's that supposed to mean?" she demanded sharply, tired of hiding the way she felt. "That I'll say 'yes' and 'so mote' to anything, smile and go along no matter what? Never argue, never complain?"

Neal looked more awake with every word. He ran his fingers through his hair. "What's gotten into you? Did somebody put hot peppers in your wash water?"

"Nothing." Kel slammed her bowl onto her tray and carried it to the servants.

Neal stopped her at the mess door. "Did anything happen last night after you left?"

"Nothing," she said, biting off the words. "Not one gods-blest thing." She left him to finish breakfast and went back to her room for her practice jacket.

She was halfway there when Cleon stopped her. He was a third-year page, a joker who still sported a tan from days spent in his father's fields, bringing in the harvest.

"Page, I need my archer's glove," he told her with a grin. "Run to my room and fetch it." When Kel frowned at him, not wanting to be bothered just then, he flapped his hands. "Run along, now. Don't take all day. You don't want punishment duty for being late."

As far as she knew, Cleon wasn't one of Joren's friends. He was just being a pain; the broad grin on his face told her that much.

What if I refused? she wondered, even as her feet started down the hall, carrying the rest of her with them. What could he do to me?

But she didn't refuse. If I'm to be a coward when I think someone goes too far with the custom, I might as well be one all the time, she thought bitterly. She ran to do as she was bid.

She caught up to Cleon as the pages were filing into their first practice of the day, and thrust his archery glove into his face. "Very good," he said, taking it. "You know, we all thought you wouldn't last this long."

Kel stared at him, thinking, What an odd thing to say! "Last this long today, or last this long for five weeks?" she asked.

"In training. You know." He spread his arms, taking in their surroundings. "Everyone had bets on that you'd run home before a week was up." He shook his head, smiling. "You might want to run now, while you still have the strength. Lord Wyldon will never let you stay."

"He might surprise you," Kel retorted, keeping her face Yamani-smooth.

Cleon smiled oddly. "He never surprises anyone." He sauntered into the yard.

Maybe he doesn't know Lord Wyldon as well as he thinks he does, Kel thought grimly as she followed him through the gate. I have to believe that.

six

THE LANCE

Later that morning, when the pages arrived at the stable, new equipment had been placed beside their normal gear. The most important item, a saddle, boasted a high, padded front and back.

Extra hands had come to show the first-years how to handle the new items: saddle, reins, double girths, and breast collars. Kel was glad to see that the man in Peachblossom's stall was the hostler Stefan. He was no common stablehand, yet he didn't seem to mind teaching her. Once he'd put the new saddle on her gelding and fastened every strap, he removed it and told Kel to try. Peachblossom sighed and shifted on his feet, just as Kel did when she was tired of dress fittings.

"Peachblossom says you didn't want Daine changing him," Stefan remarked, eyes following Kel as she positioned the saddle.

"She wouldn't do it," wheezed Kel. The new gear was *heavy*.

"But you didn't want her to," Stefan repeated.

Kel shrugged. "It seemed bad. Like, I don't know, like taking his soul."

"Not that buckle, the one next to it," Stefan told her a minute later, pointing.

Red-faced, Kel released the strap in her fingers and picked up the right one.

"He also says you promised not to rowel him."

Kel stared at the bandy-legged hostler, not sure what he meant. Then she remembered: *rowel* was another name for the pointed star-shaped type of spur favored by many knights. "That's right," she said, checking the girths.

"How will you get him to go faster?" Stefan wanted to know.

"She gave me words to say to him," replied Kel.

Stefan nodded. "She's clever, that Daine." He cleared his throat and said gruffly, "I didn't think you'd be one for the spur. Try to mount, now."

That took practice. Kel banged her leg a few times before she managed to clear the high back. "I have to do this in *armor?*" she asked Stefan, who only grinned. Kel wriggled in the saddle, testing her ability to move once she was seated. Peachblossom waited patiently for her to settle down. "About Peachblossom—I'd like to know who treated him so badly," she added, gathering her reins.

The little man chuckled. "Don't fret about that," he replied. "Leave it to me. The one that did it, he won't abuse another mount. You have my word." He slapped Peachblossom on the rear, sending the gelding out of the stall.

Once outside, Kel leaned down and told the

horse, "I think I'll stay on his good side. Just in case."

As usual, she was the last page to reach the long riding yard. Wyldon stood just inside the gate, a row of lances set against the fence beside him. Joren stood there, too. As each page rode by, Joren passed a lance up to him. He even passed one to Neal. By the time Kel reached Joren, only one of the twelve-foot-long weapons remained. Joren ignored her and mounted his horse.

"Take it," Wyldon ordered Kel, with a sharp nod at the lance.

Leaning down, she gripped the weapon and dragged it to her. It was like a very long staff in most ways. There was an indented grip cut into the wood eighteen inches from the butt, and the wood above the grip flared out to protect the bearer's hand. This weapon should never slide out of her hold. The lance was heavier than a staff, too. Kel gritted her teeth and settled the butt of the lance on the edge of her stirrup, as Lord Wyldon did.

The pages lined up. As Kel guided Peach-blossom into line beside Seaver, Wyldon rode to stand in front of them.

"Before the immortals came, there was a clamor to cut jousting from tournaments," he said loudly. "It was said to be too risky. Even with a coromanel, a wide-faced piece, on the lance tip, to soften the impact, it was too dangerous. So few battles are fought between mounted knights, it was said. It was time to retire the lance. Tradition must change to come in step with modern times."

Wyldon turned his mount toward the far end of the field. There Kel saw five quintains—dummies painted like warriors and set on wooden posts. In place of each quintain's left arm was a wooden shield with a target circle painted on it. In place of the right arm was a pole weighted at the end by a sandbag.

Lord Wyldon braced his lance under his right arm and lowered it until it was level. Once in place, it pointed at an angle across the mare's withers, into the air on Wyldon's left.

"My lord?" asked Merric, raising a hand.

Lord Wyldon raised his eyebrows.

"Shouldn't it stick out straight in front of you, not across your saddle horn?"

The older pages chuckled; Merric turned bright red at their amusement.

"Have you seen many tournaments?" Lord Wyldon inquired.

Merric shook his head, still blushing. "None, my lord."

"I could do it that way," the training master said. "Of course, I'd point my lance into the open air at my enemy's side. I'd risk walloping my own mount in the head. I assure you, they don't care for that. And once my lance goes past my opponent, what would happen?"

Merric shook his head, speechless.

"Your horse rams your opponent's mount head on," Prince Roald said quietly. "Chances are you wouldn't be able to get him out of the way in time."

"Aim for your opponent's chest with the lance pointed straight ahead, and by the time you've hit him, you cannot turn your horse aside," Lord Wyldon told them. "Strike his shield at the right point, and the power of your blow will either break the shield or drive him all the way out of the saddle—and you can still turn your mount *away* from the enemy. Do you understand now?" he asked Merric.

The boy nodded.

"Always leave an escape route for your charger," Lord Wyldon said. He turned to face the quintain. Kicking his horse into a run, he thundered down on the target. As he neared it, he stood and leaned forward. His lance tip struck the circle painted on the quintain's shield. The dummy swung a half turn, and Wyldon thundered by. At the end of the yard, he turned his bay gelding, riding back to the line of pages.

"What is the best defense for a lone knight against a giant?" he cried.

"The lance!" shouted the older pages.

"What is the best defense against an ogre?" he demanded.

"The lance!" shouted all of the pages.

"What is the best defense against a spidren?" he wanted to know.

"A lance!" yelled his audience.

"Against a charging line of foot soldiers?" Now the riding master joined them, carrying his own lance.

"A lance!" cried everyone.

"If the foot soldiers aren't armed with pikes, anyway," Kel heard Neal mutter.

Kel blinked. Neal was right. Pikes were heavy spears fourteen feet or longer. Used properly, they were defeat for horsemen, who speared their mounts on the pikes before they got within striking distance of the pikemen.

Wyldon halted in front of them. "A knight these days relies on the lance as much as the sword," he said quietly. "To use it, you must perfect both horsemanship and weapon. If you hit the quintain"—he pointed to the swinging dummy— "anywhere but that target circle, you will get a buffet from the sandbag to make the lesson stick. And it must stick. Immortals and enemy infantry do not forgive mistakes."

He dismounted and waved a fourth-year page to a line of chalk drawn across the near end of the yard. "I want you new lads up on this line. Watch the older ones as they charge. Notice they change position as they approach the target. See how the lance is couched, and gripped."

The first-years obeyed. They watched sharply as page after page took his place on the line, settled his lance, and set his horse at the quintain. The fourth-year pages hit their target almost every time, but the younger the rider, the more likely it was that the sandbag would spin around and thump him as he rode by. At last it was the turn of the first-year pages. Kel grew more and more nervous, wiping sweaty palms on her sturdy practice clothes. She knew before he struck the target that

Neal would miss the circle. She covered her eyes as the sandbag thudded into his back. At least he couldn't be knocked out of the new saddle and onto the ground.

We thank the gods for the blessings we have, she thought gloomily, and toed Peachblossom over to the chalk line. Behind her the senior pages lined up. They would ride at the quintain again once she was done.

Wyldon strode over briskly. He resettled Kel's grip on the lance with impersonal hands, checked her saddle, and stood away at last. "The lance will slide back when you strike," he told her as he'd told the other first-years. "Let it. Now, lower it across your chest, till it points out over your mount's left shoulder. Once it's down, keep that point level!"

Kel struggled to raise the lance. It was quite happy to be lowered, and agonizingly hard to raise.

"Go!" ordered Wyldon.

Kel leaned forward, her back and shoulder muscles protesting as she fought to keep the lance tip from sagging. "Charge," she ordered Peach-blossom.

The gelding took off, his speed thrusting Kel against the back of her saddle.

"Get your point up! Get it up!" cried Wyldon in a battlefield roar that cut through the thunder of Peachblossom's hooves. "Raise your *point!*"

Kel fought the weapon and her fear of the horse. Never had she suspected that a full gallop on Peachblossom would feel like riding an avalanche. I should have just said, "Go faster," she thought weakly as the target loomed. Wrestling with the lance, she just clipped the shield's edge. The quintain spun. The sandbag crashed into her side as Peachblossom thundered by.

Kel dragged on the reins as hard as she would have the day before. Peachblossom, already slowing, reared in protest against the pain in his newly soft mouth. The back on the jousting saddle kept her in her seat, just barely. Peachblossom walked backward, doing his best to keep her from falling. Kel loosened the reins, taking the pressure off the bit. Slowly the horse dropped until all four feet were planted firmly on the ground.

Kel leaned forward, the weight of her lance dragging at her arm. "I'm sorry," she whispered to the gelding. "I forgot your mouth. I won't do it again."

"The horse is too big for that page," someone called. "I'm surprised you let him ride that gelding, Cavall."

Kel wilted. The pages had learned to ignore onlookers in the practice yards. She hadn't even noticed that an audience had gathered or thought that anyone in the audience might care enough to comment.

"The probationer picked that mount herself, Goldenlake," replied Wyldon coldly. "She had a choice of horses, just like the others."

Humiliated, Kel braced her lance on her stirrup—once it was upright, she could control the wretched thing—and turned Peachblossom.

A squad of warriors mounted on fine horses

watched from outside the yard's fence. They wore the chain mail, blue and silver tunic, and white desert burnoose of the King's Own, the crown's elite guard.

Kel wished she could just sink into the ground and prayed that her Yamani schooling kept the humiliation out of her face. These men were as admired as knights, and they had seen her disgraceful try. Most were grinning.

One of them, a very tall, big man with rosy cheeks and black eyes, stared at Kel. "This is the girl?" he asked, startled. It was he who had commented to Wyldon.

The training master grimaced. "Keladry of Mindelan. She knows she may exchange her mount for another, and has chosen not to do so. Have you something we may assist you with?"

The big man shook his head. "Not this time. We've reports of a lone tauros sighted near one of the fishing villages upriver."

Kel was trying to remember what a tauros was when a Bazhir with the squad commented dryly, "No doubt it is a strayed bull."

That's it, Kel remembered. Tauroses were creatures with bull's heads and men's bodies, huge, witless monsters who preyed on women.

"Stray bull or not, we'll handle it," said the big rider. "You and your lot will get the chance to help us soon enough, Cavall." He touched his fingers to his forehead in an ironic salute, and rode off at the front of the squad.

"If we may proceed?" Wyldon asked the pages.

"You will have plenty of chances to gawk at Raoul of Goldenlake in the future."

Kel bit the inside of her cheek. Raoul of Goldenlake was the Knight Commander of the King's Own, one of the realm's finest warriors.

Neal rode over to her. "Are you all right? You have the oddest look on your face."

Kel shook her head. "I'm just embarrassed. I don't suppose you know how to make people vanish."

"It's not something they teach healers," he said dryly, riding to the starting line with her. "If I could, I'd do it all the time. Don't fret. Nobody hits the mark their first day."

"But in front of Sir Raoul of Goldenlake," she replied in a low voice. "Who fought a giant *on foot* and won."

"Actually, he's Lord Sir Raoul of Goldenlake and Malorie's Peak—the king elevated him to the peerage in April," Neal informed her. "And it was only a twenty-foot giant."

"Oh, well, I don't feel half so stupid now," muttered Kel. Time to change the subject. "What was that about us helping the King's Own?"

"The Stump likes us to get battle experience against immortals. If there's something close by, the King's Own takes us along."

Wyldon called, "You older pages practice separately. Get to it." They drifted to the other four quintains, leaving the first-years to practice under Wyldon's eye.

Wyldon beckoned to Quinden of Marti's Hill,

indicating he should tilt next. "Excuse me, your lordship, but am I older or younger today?" Neal asked.

"One day I will tie that insolent tongue of yours in a knot," replied Wyldon absently as he watched Quinden settle his lance. "You may tilt with the first-years."

Kel saw Neal open his mouth to reply, and swung Peachblossom into Neal's brown mare. The mare skipped away as Peachblossom half turned, ensuring that the gelding caught just a fold of Neal's practice clothes in his teeth instead of Neal's right leg. By the time Kel had persuaded her mount to release her friend, Neal had forgotten whatever answer he'd been about to give the training master.

Kel rode four more times at the quintain. Each try was a fight with the heavy lance; not once did she manage to keep the point high enough to strike the circle. By her third run, her arms felt as weak as overcooked noodles. Kel dragged as she brushed Peachblossom, cleaned her new tack, cut her name onto her lance, and rubbed oil into it. Only when those chores were done could she return to the castle and her waiting bath.

"What's wrong?" Neal asked as they stood in line for lunch. "You've been quiet all day, not that you ever chatter." He peered at her so worriedly that Kel had to smile.

"I didn't sleep well, that's all," she told him. "I'm sorry I was grumpy."

"Stop pushing, Esmond!" growled someone behind her. The next minute Kel was knocked out of line. Turning, she saw that the one who'd bumped her was Merric. Beet-red, he mumbled an apology and shoved Esmond in revenge. It gave him a reason to turn his back on Kel as she resumed her place.

He can't even look at me, she thought miserably, leaning against the wall. And I can't look at him. Wonderful.

She was leaving to collect her books and papers when Cleon stopped her once again. "Page Keladry," he announced with a broad grin, "my flower, my dove, I need more ink. Run along to stores and fetch me some."

"Leave her be, Cleon," said Neal sternly. "She's got enough to worry about without doing your errands."

Cleon stared at him. The senior pages were always cautious when it came to Neal. First-year or not, he was older and taller than all of them, and once he lost his temper, he didn't seem to care if he got hurt. Boys who thought nothing of pushing someone like Kel, Merric, or the other first-years around tended to leave Neal alone. "I didn't ask you, Neal," Cleon retorted at last. "She has to get used to running errands sometime."

"Even the nobles hardly ask us to do things for them," argued Neal hotly. "They know we're kept trotting."

Kel ran to do as she was told, shaking her head. Trust Neal to extend the whole matter by debating about it.

She made it to their first class just in time, handing Cleon his ink as she rushed to her seat. Only when she was down and had begun to sort out the mess of her own books and papers did she see how little she'd finished the night before. When Master Yayin, who taught reading and writing, requested her work, she stood and admitted that she didn't have it, as tradition demanded.

The Mithran's thick brows came together in a scowl. "Very well, Page Keladry," he said, "report to us orally on the chapter you were to write about."

Kel swallowed hard, fighting to keep her feelings out of her face. "I did not read it, Master Yayin," she replied, staring past him.

"No sense arguing with a Lump," someone at the back of the room muttered.

"Silence!" the teacher snapped. His favored prop was a long wooden rod he used as a pointer. In the first week of classes, Kel had learned that the rod also indicated the teacher's moods. Now he tapped its point slowly and steadily on the floor.

Bad sign, thought Kel, damp at her temples and palms. Very bad sign.

"Page Keladry, have you an explanation?"

Custom dictated only one reply. Explanations were regarded as excuses. I am stone, Kel reminded herself. "No, Master Yayin." She squeezed the words out of a tight throat.

"Page Keladry, if you cannot perform a modicum of the work required, you do not belong here," the teacher informed her coldly. "Reconsider your commitment to your studies. Tomorrow you will summarize the next three chapters in the book. Sit down."

Kel sat. She could hear snickers from the other pages, but she kept her face as smooth as stone.

In mathematics, she winced when she saw how creased and blotted her sheet of last night's problems was. She handed it in anyway, and sat through class with shoulders hunched, waiting for a reprimand. Master Ivor liked to correct their work at his desk as one of them solved a problem on a large slate in front of the room; somehow he did both easily. Papers, with his written comments, were handed back at the end of the class. He gave Kel hers with raised eyebrows, then passed to the next student. She looked down and read the note he'd scrawled on the cleanest part of the paper: "I hardly believe this is yours. Redo it, *properly*, with tonight's assignment."

She could have kissed him, she was so relieved. At least he did not want to humiliate her, even though she'd disappointed him. Since mathematics was her favorite class, she hated the idea that he might think her lazy.

Sir Myles did not assign written work, only reading, and didn't call on Kel for anything. The thought that he might kept her nervous through the class—she couldn't even remember what he'd assigned until the boys he did call on talked about the material. On her way out of class, Sir Myles asked, "Keladry? Might I have a word?"

"He probably wants to know what the Yamani

emperor has for breakfast," Neal muttered out of the side of his mouth.

Kel frowned at her friend and walked up to the plump teacher's desk. It took an effort of will to keep her hands flat at her sides, not twisting nervously together. "Is everything well?" Sir Myles wanted to know. "You look wan."

"Sir?" she asked, puzzled by the word and wondering why he'd singled her out.

"Tired, pale. Exhausted. Are you getting enough rest? The boys aren't hounding you, are they?"

Kel shook her head nervously. "No, sir. I'm fine. Couldn't be better."

His beautifully curved eyebrows rose. "And of course it would be shameful of you to say otherwise."

Here, at least, Kel was on firm ground. "Yes, sir."

"A page must endure everything that comes."

"Yes, sir." At last—answers that she knew!

"And where did you learn this?" Myles inquired mildly. "From Sir Wyldon, that paragon of knightly virtue?"

Kel frowned. Was Sir Myles being sarcastic? "I learned it from my brothers, and from the emperor's warriors, at the Yamani imperial court. Sir."

The eyebrows lifted another quarter of an inch; Myles tilted his head to one side. He reminded Kel of the sparrow Crown, who had pecked her nose that morning. Suddenly her gloom lifted a touch; she ducked her head to hide a smile.

"What does it take to be a Yamani warrior?" Myles inquired. He seemed genuinely interested.

"It takes a great deal of running up and down mountains in the rain, and not complaining about it," Kel said instantly, then clapped her hand over her mouth. What if he thought she was being impudent? But there was something about him, a sort of waiting kindness that made her want to answer him frankly.

To her relief, Myles chuckled. "I've heard of this odd behavior," he admitted. "But you admire the Yamanis."

"Oh, yes, sir!" she replied, nodding. "They keep going through *anything*."

Myles sighed. "It's my misfortune to be dumped amid so many warrior stoics," he remarked, shaking his head.

"Sir?" she asked, confused. That sounded like the best company in the world.

"Never mind. Run along to Master Lindhall. And, Keladry—"

She turned halfway to the door. "Sir?"

"If you need a friend—if you need someone to talk to—the servants can tell you where to find me."

She stared at him for a moment. The Lioness's adoptive father was offering *her* friendship!

"Thank you, sir," she said, and bowed deeply.

Myles waved her on.

Somehow Kel got through the rest of the

afternoon without further mishap. She'd completed her night's work for Master Lindhall and Tkaa the basilisk, and could hand it in with a free conscience. In etiquette Master Oakbridge was still using her as a secondary teacher of Yamani manners, and had not assigned other work to her. She had no awkward excuses to make to him.

As she changed into a dress for supper, memories of her flight from Joren and his friends, kept at bay by exercise and worry about classwork, came rushing back. Angry with herself, she picked up the practice glaive she'd brought from home and did a series of quick exercises with it. When she finished, her arms—already tired from that morning's work with the lance—were trembling. It was time to go to the mess hall.

Enough fussing, she ordered herself. Next time I'll just say something, is all. Even if it's against tradition. I won't have another day when I go around feeling like a whipped dog because I turned my back on Merric!

At supper, Prince Roald and Neal discussed the problems they'd been set in mage training while Kel considered her problem with the lance. Her second-oldest brother, Inness, had told her loftily that a girl's arms were not as strong as a boy's. After that morning she had to agree. All of the other first-year pages had been able to keep their lances from pointing at the ground.

I have to train harder, decided Kel. I have to strengthen my arms.

She fiddled with her spoon, wondering if she'd

ever be able to lift that cursed lance. Then Joren's voice rang out across the room: "I swear, those Shang warriors have an exercise for *everything*."

"If you wish to be a herald, Joren, apply to their college in the morning," Wyldon said, raising his own voice. "Until then, converse in a more seemly way."

A brief hush fell. As Wyldon gave the signal to rise, Neal asked her, "Are you studying with us tonight?"

"In a while," she promised. "Do you know where I might find the Wildcat?" For once, Joren had helped her. If anyone would know how to strengthen her arms, it would be a Shang warrior who spent her life fighting men.

She had to try a couple of the places Neal and Roald suggested, but was successful at last. Eda Bell was happy to show Kel exercises for the arms. The hardest involved lying flat on the ground, pushing the body up with both arms, lowering it partway, then pushing up again. Kel managed only three of these exercises under the Wildcat's eye before her exhausted arms gave out. Eda promised her that if she kept exercising, she would do better soon. Feeling hopeful, Kel headed back to the pages' wing.

seven

KEL TAKES A STAND

For the next three days Kel pursued her classwork and physical training doggedly. When Sunday came at last, she and the other pages attended dawn worship for Mithros, the god of warriors and the sun. After that she gave her weapons and tack an extra cleaning for Lord Wyldon's inspection just before lunch. When he finished going over every inch of a page's equipment, he gave punishment assignments for the penalties collected during the week.

Kel had been late to one class, to one meal, and to the riding corral the day before, when Peachblossom had been grumpier than usual. For each of those tardy arrivals Lord Wyldon issued her work in the pages' armory for one bell of time, consuming her entire afternoon. All of the other pages had punishment duty, too. Merric and Olin fared worse than Kel. They had to work all afternoon and for a bell on Sunday night.

"I'd like to find whoever taught the Stump that extra work builds character and push him down the stairs," Neal told Kel at lunch.

She smiled and returned to solving a puzzle. How was she to do her classwork for Monday if she was cleaning armor? At last she hit on a plan and bore her work to the armory. First, she rolled chain mail in barrels full of sand to scour away dirt, until she wearied. Then she attacked her assignments. At her first yawn Kel returned to cleaning. When the supper bell rang, she had scoured a large amount of mail and finished nearly all of her classwork. After an evening of staff practice with Neal, she knew she had used the day well, and went to bed content.

Monday came soon enough. By nightfall she was exhausted and wishing for another Sunday. Then Cleon, grinning hugely, caught her after supper and asked her to fetch some books from the Mithrans' library, in a separate wing of the palace. She could see he was waiting for her to refuse so he could say she thought herself better than the other first-years. With a sigh, she trotted off to do as she was bid.

Tuesday was more of the same. Only her sparrows' reaction to her arm-strengthening exercises—they lined up on her windowsill like spectators at a tournament—made Kel smile that day. At tilting practice later that morning she managed to hit Peachblossom's head and the quintain dummy, but not the target shield. The laughter of pages and onlookers rang in her ears, but she kept her feelings hidden. By the time she rode Peachblossom back to the stable in the wake of the other pages, she wanted to crawl into a dark corner and die.

Kel was the last to finish grooming her mount and the last to finish looking after her tack. By the time she tended her weapons, the other pages had gone; she had to hurry if she was to bathe before lunch. Working in haste, she dropped her lance. It clattered across the stable floor, collecting dirt along its freshly oiled length. As it rolled, a small button of wood fell away, revealing a dark hole.

Kel stared at the spot, wanting to cry. Now she would have to polish the lance again and find some way to fill the gap. Bending down, she picked up the piece that had fallen out. It wasn't a splintered chunk, but a perfectly cut plug two inches wide. The sides were sawed clean, tapering inward.

That's odd, she thought. Picking up the lance, she looked for the hole left by the missing piece. It was stark against the light brown of the wood because there was something black at its bottom.

Kel stuck her little finger inside and scraped the dark substance. Inspecting the stuff under her nail, she realized it was lead.

Now she went over the entire lance, not with her callused fingertips but with the more sensitive pads of her fingers. There were five more plugs spaced along the length of wood. She pried them out; each hid a hollow filled with lead. They were placed so that no part of the staff was out of balance with the rest. It had been cleverly done, the plugs replaced to match the grain of the lance and the whole polished until the cuts were nearly invisible.

Kel lifted the other pages' lances. All weighed

much less than her own.

Fury pounded at her temples and behind her eyes. Was this what Cleon had meant when he'd said to run while she still had a chance? She pictured the big redhead and sighed. No. He was the kind who would shove someone into a puddle. This sort of trickery would be too much work for Cleon.

Getting her lance, Kel stuck the first plug back into its socket. She began to oil and polish the wood anew, thinking. Had Neal known about this? She tried to remember if she'd ever seen him touch her lance. No, he hadn't, nor had Wyldon, she remembered. Joren had been the only one to handle it before it got to Kel. Custom dictated that Kel alone would touch it once it was hers.

Kel was sure that Joren wouldn't be the only one who knew. The joke was too good to keep to himself. He would have needed a palace carpenter, too. None of the pages would be able to do the kind of fine work the trick lance required. Enough warriors trained with weighted arms that a carpenter would think nothing of putting lead into a practice lance.

Kel thought about it through her bath, and took her time scrubbing. Normally she rushed so no one had to wait long to eat, but today she did not feel kindly toward her fellow pages. For once she would have a proper wash and they could listen to their growling bellies for a while. If extra work was the price she paid to remind them that she could disrupt their lives, too, she would pay it gladly.

When Kel reached the mess hall, the waiting pages and squires growled. She put on her most Yamani-Lump expression and got her food. She knew it infuriated those who disliked her when she appeared not to care if they even existed. On a day like today when, fairly or unfairly, she disliked most of the pages, she positively enjoyed letting them think she cared for their opinions not one whit.

"A word after lunch, probationer," Wyldon called as she looked around for Neal.

Kel bowed to him, found Neal, and took her seat. Wyldon's prayer, to "perform our duties quickly and promptly," did not even make her twitch. Neither did his after-lunch order to report to the armory on Sunday for two bells' worth of labor. She bowed politely to the training master in reply, and ran to catch up with her friends.

"Are you all right?" Prince Roald wanted to know as they walked to their afternoon classes. "You're being quiet even for you."

Kel glanced up. Both Roald and Neal were looking at her. She was certain that Neal didn't know about the lance, but what about the prince? He was one of Joren's year-mates. Despite his joining her and Neal from time to time, she wasn't sure what he thought of her.

Finally she decided that Roald didn't know. Joren had begun in the same year as the prince, but Roald, who was careful to eat with all of the pages so no one felt jealous, spent the least amount of time with Joren and his cronies.

Should she tell them? She knew that Neal was her friend and she thought the prince might be.

No. Yamanis did not whine about what was fair or unfair, and she was too much a Yamani still. She would not let anyone think she could not handle whatever got dished out to her.

Kel shook her head in answer to the prince's query. "I haven't anything to say."

"Dear girl, we noticed," drawled Neal in his most scholarly-elegant way.

Kel ignored him and returned to her complicated thoughts. What if she kept the lance? If she mastered it, the bigger lances of the knights would be easy to handle.

The afternoon passed. Kel reported to classes as usual. She also studied each of her fellow pages, trying to guess which of them had been in on Joren's trick.

At supper, she ate lightly. Given her plans for the evening, a full stomach was a bad idea. Going straight to her room, she changed from her dress to practice clothes. It was time to stop playing the shy newcomer. She listened as the boys returned to their rooms to collect their study materials. When Neal rapped on her door, she pretended she wasn't in until he went away.

Finally no more steps sounded in the pages' wing. Kel left her room to walk the corridors. She made no sound in her soft leather slippers, ghosting along as she had been taught in the Islands, listening hard.

Passing the pages' main library, she heard the slam of a heavy book striking the floor. "Pick that up for me, will you, Merric?" The voice was Joren's.

Kel stopped outside the open door. Her heart drummed in her chest.

"Yessir, Page Joren," she heard Merric say dully. Peeking through the crack in the door, Kel saw Merric place a fat volume on the table next to the blond page.

As he did, Zahir shoved another heavy book off the table. "Pick it up," said Vinson of Genlith, cackling with mirth. "Can't have books on the floor."

Merric stared at the older boys with resentment, then got the book.

Joren immediately pushed his volume off the table. As Merric stared at him, Joren then lifted a stack of smaller books with a taunting smile. His eyes never left Merric's as he let them drop one by one onto the floor.

Kel's stomach tightened. She took a deep breath and walked into the library.

"This is wrong," she said, halting in front of the blond page.

"Oh, look—it's the Lump." On the other side of the table Vinson got to his feet. "Do you want trouble, probationer?" he asked, grinning. "We'd just *loooove* to give it to you."

"No, I don't want it," Kel replied. She kept her eyes on Joren. The leader of a gang was always the one to watch. The others would take their cues from him. "What I want is for you to stop pushing the first-years around."

Joren stared at her, his blue eyes bright. "I see," he said in a thoughtful tone. "We haven't gotten rid of you yet, so you think you're accepted. Merric, pick up those books."

"Don't, Merric," Kel said, still watching Joren.

"It's custom," the redheaded boy muttered.

"Not like this, it's not," replied Kel. "Us fetching and carrying gloves and armor polish, that's enough. Forcing people to mop with their clothes and pick up things dropped on purpose has nothing to do with being a page."

Joren laughed softly, shaking his head. "Oh, this is too much," he said at last. "The Yamani Lump—our very temporary annoyance—will school us in proper behavior."

"I shouldn't have to," Kel told him. "You should know how a true knight behaves."

A hand clamped around the back of her neck: Zahir's. She hadn't even heard him get out of his chair.

"Shall I take the Lump away?" the Bazhir inquired of Joren.

Gripping Zahir's index finger, Kel jammed her thumbnail into the base of Zahir's own nail. The experience, she knew very well, was a painful one.

He yelped and let go. Joren lunged for her.

She stepped back, ducking under Zahir's frantic punch. Instead, the Bazhir hit Joren. Kel backed up to reach the open center of the library.

Merric, to her relief, had fled. She was glad not to have to worry about him.

Zahir was cursing and coddling his fist; his punch had connected solidly with Joren's skull. Joren rubbed the spot where his friend had struck as he walked toward Kel. He was crimson with rage. Vinson was nowhere to be seen.

Something clattered behind Kel. In spite of herself, she looked. Vinson had fallen over a footstool as he emerged from the shelves at her rear.

She turned back quickly. Joren was leaping straight at her.

Kel's Yamani training took over. She grabbed Joren's tunic and turned, kneeling as she did. He went flying over her shoulder, just as the Yamani ladies had done during their practices together. The ladies, however, did not hit a long study table on their bellies, sliding along its polished length to crash headfirst into a bookshelf.

A foot slammed into her back between her shoulder blades. Zahir had recovered. Kel rolled forward as she went down, to fetch up against the legs of the table she'd just polished with Joren. Zahir moved in to kick her; she seized his booted foot and twisted, growling with effort. Off balance he stumbled and fell. Kel hurled a nearby stool at him. He rolled, covering his head with his arms.

Then Vinson gripped her ankles, dragging her forward. Kel sat up and grabbed his hands. Someone grasped her hair from behind and yanked her to the floor again. Ignoring the pain as the hair-puller kept his grip, Kel rolled away from a punch. She clung to his wrists to keep him from yanking out a chunk of hair. The roll twisted her out of Vinson's hold on her legs. She kicked out, slamming her feet into Vinson's belly. That hand in her hair yanked, dragging her into the middle of the floor. Her grim-faced captor was Joren.

Kel felt his wrist and dug her thumbnails into the soft flesh between the bones. He cursed and let go.

Lunging to her feet, Kel ran into Zahir. Grinning, the Bazhir punched her in the stomach. When her scant supper came up, she made sure he got most of it. Another solid blow from Joren connected with her back, spinning her around. His second punch hit her face just as Vinson grabbed her.

Next time, she thought fiercely, hooking Joren's leg with her foot and yanking, next time I'll make sure I've got my back to the wall!

Vinson was the last of the older pages to walk out of Lord Wyldon's study. Through the open door Kel heard the training master call, "Send her in."

"Here, milord," announced the man who waited on Lord Wyldon in the evenings. Holding the door as Kel passed, he winked at her in encouragement.

Kel halted in front of Lord Wyldon's desk as the door closed. The training master inspected her and shook his head. Kel knew she looked dreadful. From her past experience she knew she had a black eye and a puffy lip. Her nose was probably broken.

A trickling on her cheeks told her the splits in both of her eyebrows were bleeding.

"Blot that," Wyldon ordered, and thrust his handkerchief across his desk. Kel stared as if he had offered a foreign object, then reached for it stiffly. Her left arm hurt. The skin on her knuckles was torn and bleeding on both hands.

"Would you care to explain?" Wyldon picked up a large cup and sipped from it.

"Sir?" she asked thickly.

"How were you injured? As I recall, you were in one piece earlier tonight."

She tried to breathe through her nose, and winced. "I fell down, Lord Wyldon," she said carefully. Lifting the handkerchief from her cut, she examined it with her good eye, and pressed the clean linen to the split in the other brow.

"*What* did you say, probationer?"

His tone made her stiffen. She tried to stand tall and put her hands behind her back, as they were expected to when questioned. The left arm only went so far before pain made her dizzy.

"Never mind that," snapped Wyldon. "Answer me."

"I fell," she replied evenly. At least she didn't have to worry about making up a lie, when time-honored custom had already supplied her with one.

Wyldon fiddled with his tea mug. "Come, come, girl. You were in a fight. Name those you fought with."

"Begging your pardon, my lord, but there was

no fight," she told him. "I fell down."

"You fought with Joren, Zahir, and Vinson," Wyldon reminded her.

"Did they say that?" asked Kel, her face as blank as any true-born Yamani's. "How strange. *I* fell down."

Wyldon stared. "I imagine you have now come to your senses and wish to go home. At this time of year that will be difficult—"

Surprised enough to forget her manners, she interrupted him. "No, sir."

"It will not be difficult? For your information, it has been snowing in the north over the past two weeks. It will snow here tonight." Wyldon rubbed his healing arm.

"No, sir," Kel repeated firmly. "I don't want to go home. Your lordship."

"You do not want to go home." If she hadn't believed he could never be startled, she might have thought that he was now. He didn't normally repeat simple ideas.

"I don't believe falling down is an offense for which I can be expelled," she said, trying to speak clearly. "I still have the rest of the year to prove myself."

Wyldon tapped his fingers on his desk. "You have the armory Sunday afternoons until April," he said at last. "And an essay each week on the improper uses of combat training. Now you'd better see a palace healer. That nose looks broken. Dismissed."

Kel bowed stiffly, then remembered something. She held out his handkerchief.

"Have it washed and returned to me," Wyldon ordered.

"Very good, my lord," she replied, and left. Neal would tell her where the healers saw patients.

Duke Baird of Queenscove, chief of the realm's healers, was a tall, weary-looking man. A dark gray over-robe protected the black velvet tunic and hose he wore in mourning for the two sons he had lost. His eyes were a darker green than Neal's, set deep under straight brows. There was a red tint to his brown hair that was absent in his son's, but they had the same nose and the same direct gaze. While Neal paced, Baird rested big hands on Kel's shoulders. She saw his magic as emerald-colored light around his hands, and she felt it as a cool tide through her body. Her stiffness eased; the edge came off her aches. Kel had been beaten up before, but never so thoroughly; it shamed her to feel so happy at the easing of pain. The warriors at the imperial court had always insisted they did not even pay attention to pain when they had it.

Baird let go of her and rubbed his hands. "I am impressed, young lady," he told her with a wry smile. "You have been royally pounded."

Kel smiled at him. "You should see the other fellows."

"There!" cried Neal, holding up his hands. "You see what I have to deal with!"

"You may have noticed my son has an endless

capacity for drama," Baird told Kel.

She couldn't help it: she grinned, and winced as her split lip opened.

"Ah," said the healer duke, "we can't have this." He touched an icy finger to Kel's lip. The hurt vanished. Next he touched the cuts in her eyebrows and on her hands; they went cold, then painless. The swellings on her knuckles shrank. Scraped places scabbed, as if Duke Baird had put three days' worth of healing into her.

"So much for chivalrous ideals, eh?" Neal demanded. "Three pages in their third year of training jump a first-year—a first-*season* page—"

"I started it," Kel informed her friend.

"Tell me another," he snapped.

"I did, on my honor." Kel looked at Neal's father. "I think Lord Wyldon just wanted my nose seen to, your grace. Not the rest."

"Since he sent you without written instructions, I may exercise my judgment," Baird told her. "I will indeed see to your nose. You've also pulled muscles in your left side—I can mend that and reduce the swelling around your eye. It will not do if you were to miss training because you could not see. I can also ease that headache."

"What possessed you?" demanded Neal. He seemed as vexed by this matter-of-fact discussion as by Kel's story. "Why in the name of all the gods in all the Eastern and Southern Lands would you start a fight with them?"

Kel sighed. She wasn't about to tell how

Merric had been shamed. "I didn't like the shape of Joren's nose."

Neal stared at her, eyes bulging. Finally he said, "If you meant to impress the Stump, you wasted your time. Don't you realize he'll never let you stay?"

Kel looked down. "He could change his mind," she insisted. "You always think the worst of him."

"I *what?*" Neal began to produce a series of outraged noises that included squawks and whistling inhaled breaths. He sounded like one of her young nephews having a tantrum, not like a fifteen-year-old who'd been raised at court and at the university.

"If you cannot be quiet while I work," his father told him patiently, "go into the waiting room."

Neal marched out. A moment later, they heard him arguing with himself. Duke Baird closed the examining room door and placed his hands on either side of Keladry's head. "This may sting a bit," he warned.

"Sting" was not the word Kel would have used to describe the healing of her broken nose. The flesh around it moved; cartilage grated. Her sinuses and teeth ached sharply, then throbbed. The pain stopped abruptly. She could breathe again.

She could also see from both eyes. The ache in her left side was fading. A moment later, Duke Baird stepped away from her.

"Beautiful," he said with approval. "You're quite strong, you know. I couldn't have done nearly so much if you weren't in the pink of health to begin with. You didn't fight me, either. You made it easy."

"My mother cracked us on the head with her fan when we fought healers," Kel admitted. "We all decided it was better to let them do their work."

"The Ilane of Seabeth and Seajen I used to dance with was a most forthright young lady," Baird admitted, smiling. "I am glad to see that she still is."

Now it was Kel's turn to gape. Her mother used to dance? With men who were not her father?

"I hope you will remember me to her when next you write." Baird helped her to slide off his examining table.

"Yes, sir. I mean, yes, your grace," Kel said, fumbling the proper words for a man of his rank.

Baird opened the door to his waiting room. Neal stood in the middle of it, hands on hips. "I've decided," Neal announced. "She's insane. The entire palace is insane."

His father lifted reddish-brown eyebrows. "Does this mean that you have come to your senses and will return to the university?" he asked mildly.

Neal choked, glared at his father, and stalked out of the room.

"I didn't think so," Baird remarked softly. "Keladry, I would like to say I hope we only meet socially in future. Somehow, I don't think that will be the case."

Kel grinned at him. "You're probably right, your grace."

"Don't mind my boy. He gets…overenthusiastic, but he has a good heart."

"I know *that*," Kel reassured the duke, and yawned.

"To bed," the healer ordered. "You need the sleep."

Kel bowed, covering another yawn, and trotted to catch up with Neal.

⇥ eight ⇤

WINTER

*T*he next morning Kel opened her eyes to discover it was not yet dawn. She moaned. Once, just *once*, it would have been nice to sleep through the bell to Gower's knock on her door. Even with a banked fire her room was icy, a solid argument for staying abed until the last possible moment. She probably shouldn't do her morning exercises until tomorrow or the next day. Even with Duke Baird's treatment, she ached all—

Several somethings hopped on her chest, interrupting her thoughts. Kel looked down.

Thirteen sparrows, the entire courtyard flock, stood on the coverlet. Crown hopped up the distance from Kel's navel to somewhere below her chin, where Kel lost sight of her. She closed her eyes, waiting for the gentle peck.

Instead the quick gait that circled her cheek stopped beside her ear. "PEEP!"

Kel sat up, startling the birds into flight. They perched on the headboard, chattering at her.

"Wonderful," she said, throwing off the covers.

"So much for a little extra sleep." Looking up, she saw one of the small shutters was open. No wonder the room was cold. She hobbled stiffly to the window, mumbling, "How can a tiny bird produce such a loud noise?"

She opened the bottom shutters. Outside, the pre-dawn world was white. Over a foot of snow had fallen in the courtyard. More continued to fall in a steady, business-like way. It muffled all sound, making Kel feel as if she and the birds were wrapped in a thick down comforter.

"I see why you came in," she said, turning to look at her guests. They had taken advantage of her departure to huddle in the warm hollow she'd left in her mattress. Kel grinned, and went to poke up the fire. Once she had it going, she lit a branch of candles and carried them into her dressing room. Overhead the great bell called everyone to another day's work.

With no hearth, the dressing room was icy. Kel danced on the bare stone flags, teeth chattering as she stripped off her nightgown. A colorful sight awaited her: fading yellow-purple bruises spread over her left side and mottled her legs. A bigger, red-purple bruise was just surfacing on her belly. Kel whistled, impressed in spite of herself. She had to have been in one or two worse fights than this, although they slipped her mind at the moment. The marks vanished under her clothes as she drew on her undertunic and scarlet wool hose. By that point she was shivering so badly that it was all she could do to feed the laces through the holes in the long garments. She was securing the hose to her undertunic when she heard a rap on her door.

"Just a moment," she called, grabbing a robe. Wishing that servants could simply enter her room and knowing the boys would destroy her things if she had the special locks removed, she ran to open the door. Gower took two steps past her with his tray, then turned to stare.

"Sunrise come early today, miss?"

Kel blinked at him. "What?"

The man nodded to her face. "Looks like the sun's about to come up in your eye. Nice color."

"Thank you, I think."

He put down the tray and saw the birds perched close to the fire. "Time was a man didn't have to deal with wild animals in the palace," he commented.

"They aren't wild, exactly," she protested as he left the room, closing the door.

The sparrows cheeped. Kel emptied a cup of the seed she had begged from the stables weeks before onto her desk. Dumping her collection of colored rocks from their shallow dish, she filled it with water and put it down for the birds. That done, she hurried to wash and finish dressing. Looking at her face in the mirror, she saw what Gower had meant: the swelling was gone, but she had brightly colored bruises around one eye and her other eyebrow and on one cheekbone. Kel shook her head and left her room.

Turning around after she locked up, she nearly tripped over Merric. He shoved her. "I didn't ask you to come bullocking in!" he yelled. "I don't need you to defend me!"

Kel held up her hands and stepped back. "I didn't do it for you," she told him.

"Now they'll give me all kinds of grief, saying I got a *girl* to—hunh?"

Kel sighed. "I didn't do it for you, all right? I wanted to pick a fight with them and you were there, that's all."

The noise was drawing other pages out of their rooms.

"Just leave me alone!" Merric yelled, uncomfortably aware of their audience. He punched Kel in the left arm, then the right, as if daring her to hit back.

The blows hurt, but she let him have them. His pride was sore; she understood that. Her parents had explained it, the first few times that someone she had tried to help got angry with her. She wished that Merric had tried to hit his tormentors as well. He wouldn't be so angry if he'd gotten in a punch or two of his own last night.

"Just because you're a stupid probationer *girl* doesn't mean you can ignore custom like that, either!" Merric informed her.

Kel sighed again. She had been patient enough—she wanted her breakfast. "Like I said, it had nothing to do with you." Tucking her hands into her belt, she marched down the hall. The other boys gathered around Merric. She could hear them asking him what had happened.

She wondered what he would say. Not your

problem, she told herself, and picked up her pace. She was *hungry*.

Neal was not far behind her. "Ungrateful little swine," he muttered as he sat across from Kel.

She looked up from spooning honey onto her porridge. Never had breakfast looked so good. Healings always made her hungry. "Me?"

"No, Merric."

Kel looked down. "Oh. You heard."

"My room isn't that far from yours. He doesn't have to be your slave the rest of his life, but a little thanks—"

"And if it was you?" Kel asked, buttering a scone.

Neal blinked at her.

"Would you have thanked me?" She bit into her scone.

"Well, I—I—"

Kel swallowed. "It's bad enough Joren and his pack shamed him. Me seeing it shamed him more. Me *doing* something about it…" She dug into her porridge, letting Neal think it over.

As she ate, she looked for Joren, Zahir, and Vinson. Their appearance was much more colorful than hers. Since they hadn't broken anything, they had not been sent to a healer. Not bad work, for a first-year, she thought, careful to keep her face straight.

Neal was still thinking about what Kel had said when Salma found them. "Lord Wyldon sent me to remind you to wait on his table the next three nights," she informed Kel. "I'll have a clean uniform ready after your classes. Make sure you reach the mess before he does."

Kel nodded. Every other page had gone through the same routine.

Salma touched her bruised eye. "Nice sunrise," she commented, and smiled.

Kel grinned back.

"That's another thing," grumbled Neal. "You're *happy* about that fight."

Kel buttered another scone. "Yes."

"Great griffins, why? Do you *like* getting hurt?"

She put her butter knife down. "Don't you ever get tired of asking questions?"

"Never. They're mother's milk to me. Answer, please."

Kel toyed with her scone. She usually didn't like to explain herself, but she respected Neal. "Warriors get hurt. You don't have to like it, just live with it. And last night I got tired of thinking and worrying myself sick. I knew what had to be done, and I did it." She sighed happily. "I love it when that happens."

Before the pages left the mess hall, Lord Wyldon made an announcement. As long as the snow continued to fall, Shang combat, weapons practice, and archery would be held at the indoor practice courts.

Kel almost ran into Cleon as she headed out of the mess. He'd planted himself squarely in her path. She halted, staring at him with exasperation.

"Good morning, teardrop of my heart," he greeted her.

Kel sighed, her shoulders drooping. He wasn't a bully like Joren. Last night had been about bullies, not about a silly custom. "What is it this time?"

Cleon blinked. He'd expected a refusal. He recovered quickly. "My quiver, if you would, my pearl. I took it to my room to sharpen the arrowheads last night, and of course I will require it. Return soon to my side, or I will pine."

He'll pine and I'm a holly bush, she thought with grim good humor, trotting back to the pages' wing.

At the end of archery practice, Lord Wyldon told them that riding class was canceled. "This is true only during storms," he explained as they put away their bows. "If it is just a matter of snow on the ground, you train outdoors."

Someone groaned.

Wyldon bore down on the groaner, the first-year page named Quinden. "Do you think spidrens sit indoors in the winter?" he rapped out. "They've got nice furry coats. They don't care if it's freezing. Killer centaurs and killer unicorns hate drifts, but they'll attack in shallow snow. Get used to fighting in it." He turned to include the rest of the pages in his lecture. "Once a knight could take his ease in winter. Pirates, bandits, Scanrans, and Carthakis stayed home. We practiced our snow hunting skills, being polite to ladies, and polishing our armor. Winter was our easy season.

"These immortals changed everything," he

went on. "Many are out and about in all but the worst weather, which means we come out, too."

"But most of them returned to the Divine Realms this summer," argued a third-year. "Didn't they?"

"There are hundreds still in Tortall," Wyldon said grimly. "And hundreds more, once they breed. Only the monsters that came after Midwinter Festival last year were returned to the Divine Realms. That leaves plenty for us to deal with, one way or another. Any other questions?"

The pages shook their heads.

"Today we commence with a knight's primary weapon," Wyldon informed them. Sergeant Ezeko came forward pushing a barrel set on a small, wheeled cart. The barrel was stuffed with wooden practice swords.

"Take one," he ordered. "Treat it as your own from this moment."

No one handed a practice sword to Kel. She was able to try several before choosing one. It felt easy in her grasp, almost feather-light after her lance. The exercises were like those for the staff; the thing to remember was that the weapon was shorter. They were paired off as usual. Wyldon and Ezeko took them through the basics, high blocks against high strikes, middle strikes to middle blocks, and low blocks against low strikes. Ezeko then led the older boys in more complex exercises as Lord Wyldon stayed with the first-years. To Kel's surprise, Neal practiced with the oldest pages. As a nobleman's son he'd been tutored in the use of a sword for the last seven years.

Lord Wyldon took Neal's place in the first-year pairs, with Merric as his partner. Kel practiced with Esmond, and found she enjoyed it. Sword work was completely new, so she never had to worry about confusing it with anything she had learned in the Islands. Blocking and striking came easily. When the bell rang for the end of practice, she was sorry to quit. So was Esmond, it seemed— he actually gave her a friendly clap on the shoulder before he put away his practice sword.

After her last class, Kel trotted to her rooms, whistling cheerfully. She was tired and sore as always, but for once she was ahead of the others. It looked as if she would be cleaned up and ready to wait on Wyldon's table on time.

Once dressed in a fresh tunic, she opened her door cautiously, checking overhead for buckets and the floor for anything smelly. Locking up, Kel set off briskly. Two steps, and her feet skidded out from under her; down she went on her back. When she finally managed to get to her feet, there was oil on her clothes and in her hair. The light cast by the hall torches had not shown her oil smeared on the gray flagstones.

Back into her room she went, to wash and change clothes again. As she dressed she heard the boys leaving for supper. Now she *was* going to be late.

This time when she left her room she skirted the oil and trudged down the hall. Joren, Vinson, and Zahir waited for her near the mess hall.

"I guess you'll learn not to tattle," sneered Vinson.

"I didn't tattle," she said. "The servants told him."

"Never mind that," Joren said, glaring at Vinson. "You've had it easy, wench. That's at an end. You should have fled while you had the chance." Zahir opened the mess-hall door.

"You were going to be rid of me by now," she said, her voice ringing clear against the stone walls.

Vinson started to turn back. Joren grabbed his tunic and shoved him through the mess door.

Zahir called over his shoulder, "You won't be here come spring, *probationer*."

For her late arrival, Wyldon assigned Kel to wait on his table through the month of January. His guests that night, two grizzled warriors from the northern army, spent the meal telling jokes about women who were never prompt. Kel had to remind herself often to be as stone.

After that, she left her room to wait on Lord Wyldon by climbing through her shutters. She did it even when the drifts were high in the courtyard: snow could always be brushed off.

Six days later Midwinter Festival began, celebrating the rebirth of the sun and of the year after the longest night of winter. There was no classroom work during the week-long holiday, so the pages could ready themselves to serve in the great banquet hall for each night of the feast. Kel had dreaded her first experience of waiting on the great people of the realm, but to her relief, the first-year pages were spared the ordeal of service in the public eye. Instead she spent the banquet hours at the head of the kitchen stairs. There the first-years passed the plates of food from the servants to the second-, third-, and fourth-year pages, who actually waited on the diners.

She decided that the worst part of her chore was constantly being under the eye of Master Oakbridge, the etiquette teacher. He missed nothing, either in the banquet hall or on the stairs. No one was allowed to relax for so much as a breath as long as the feasts went on. Kel would have loved the chance to look inside the hall at the nobles and all their finery. In the Yamani Islands the holiday was spent in quiet, at home with family. The colorful celebrations of the Eastern Lands—with the great logs for the hearths, the fantastic structures of cakes and candy shaped like castles and immortals, the silk garlands, and the performances of players—were just a dim memory for her. She would have liked to see more than hot, sweaty kitchen folk and nervous, sweaty senior pages.

It was also annoying to have to wait the long hours until the pages' supper. Only after the king and queen led their guests to a ballroom were the pages released from duty. The squires got to wait on the great ones while the pages ate silently and fell into bed.

The morning after the longest night of the

year, the fourth day of the seven-day celebration, was the time when gifts were exchanged. They all took their packages to Salma so that when the servants came to lay the first fires of the year, they could also bring each page's gifts.

Kel had thought long and hard about her gifts. Neal was easy: she gave him one of her lucky cats, since he never came into her room without looking at them. "With your tongue," she wrote on her note to him, "you need all the luck you can get!"

Gower received a silver noble for the work he did in her room. Money would not have been right for Salma. Instead Kel gave her a silver hummingbird pin from her trinket box.

The prince had been a source of worry. She thought it might be presumptuous to give him a present, but she really wanted to. She gave him a small Yamani painting of a bridge over a forest stream. The colors were dreamlike: grays, faded blues and greens, stark browns. It always gave her a feeling of peace, and she hoped it would make Roald feel better about his coming marriage.

For Crown and the other sparrows she had gotten raisins and dried cherries, a rare treat for the birds. They were pecking at the fruit when Gower knocked on Kel's door.

In addition to her wash water he carried a sack containing three gifts. One came from Neal, a leather-bound volume about the female warriors who had once defended the realm of Tortall. To Kel's surprise, Prince Roald gave her a blown glass horse no longer than her thumb. When she saw the flattened ears and the bared teeth, she laughed. It looked very like Peachblossom.

There was no name on the third gift. Kel undid the crimson silk wrap to find a stone jar as broad as her palm. It was made of green jasper and the words "Bruise Balm" were carved into the stone stopper. Kel opened it and sniffed. The thick ointment inside had a delicate smell. Curious, she put a dab on a knuckle she had bruised in yesterday's hand-to-hand combat. The moment the bruise balm touched it, the ache that had plagued her all night stopped. By the time she had washed up and cleaned her teeth, the swelling had started to go down.

Neal banged on her door as she finished dressing. Kel let him in, remembering to leave the door open. "I love that little cat," he said, ruffling her hair. "Thank you."

Kel grinned. "You're welcome. Neal, who do you think sent me this?" She handed the jar to him.

Neal opened it, sniffed, and frowned. He sniffed again, then waved a hand over the jar. "Ouch!" he cried, startled. "Well, label me *very* impressed and ship me to Carthak."

"Are you hurt?" she asked. What if the ointment was some kind of nasty trick? "What happened?"

Neal replaced the lid and offered the jar back to Kel. "There's *serious* healing spelled into this," he informed her. "It's worth its weight in gold."

"But who?" Kel asked. "Who would give me such a thing?"

"Don't look at me." Neal tore up a dried cherry that had caused some disagreements among the sparrows. "I might have the skill to brew something like this in ten years, but only then. Wasn't there a note?"

Kel shook her head. She rested a hand on her belt-knife, wondering. She had never told Neal about the peerless blade with its plain sheath and hilt. Now she did, and showed him the knife.

"So maybe somebody with money and taste knows what a page needs and wants you to have it," he suggested as they went to breakfast. "Too bad they couldn't arrange to have the Stump done away with for you."

"I don't want him done away with," she told him as they walked into the mess hall. "I just want him to take me off probation."

Neal was about to reply but changed his mind. It didn't matter that he hadn't spoken.

"You watch," Kel informed him stubbornly. "I'll do so well he'll have to let me stay."

"A wish for the new year," her friend said, passing her a tray. "So mote it be."

"So mote," whispered Kel, and followed him into the line for breakfast.

With the Festival's end, winter settled in. The sparrows decided to make Kel's room their quarters. Each day they chirped what she hoped were encouraging remarks, not bird jokes, as she did her pre-dawn exercises. They even ate from her hand as well as from the shallow dishes she'd found for them. Kel was grateful that none of the servants had complained about droppings. She would have hated to give up her feathered companions. The single-spot female, Crown, was particularly devoted over the gray days and cold nights, perching on Kel's shoulder whenever the girl was in her room.

In late January, Kel was studying in the library when she noticed that Seaver had come and gone three different times in one evening. He would take a volume, return at a trot with it, and find another. The last time he searched the shelves, she closed her own book and followed him. He turned into Joren's room.

"You *still* haven't gotten it right," she heard Joren cry as Vinson giggled. "Are you deaf? We need the third book on the Hunger Wars in Galla!"

"You said it was the second volume on farming in Scanra." Kel had to strain to hear Seaver. Of all the new boys, he was the quietest. "You—ow!"

"Hit him again, Vinson," Joren advised. "Knock the wax from his ears."

Kel opened the door in time to see Vinson cuff Seaver. "Just when I finished most of my punishment work, too," she announced.

"It's the Lump," Vinson told Joren, as if the

blond youth couldn't see that for himself.

"What will it take to get through your thick skull?" Joren demanded, getting to his feet. Vinson stepped to Kel's left, so the two third-years could come at her from either side. "Perhaps we ought to break it this time."

"Where's Zahir? Did he lose the belly for your silly games?" Kel asked. "Seaver, please go."

Seaver looked from Vinson to Joren.

"Stay if you want," Joren said, his eyes on Kel. "We'll bash you, too."

Vinson kicked Seaver without warning. Kel lunged, grabbing Vinson by the tunic, and hurled him into Joren. Seaver ran out of the room as the two older pages scrambled to get Kel.

The rest went as she expected. She lost, but struck a few good blows she might not have managed earlier in the year. They all told Wyldon the traditional lie and took their punishment chores without complaint. At this rate, Kel thought, I won't have a free hour between now and summer solstice.

The next evening Kel, the prince, and Neal decided to study in Neal's room. They had just opened their books when someone knocked on the open door. It was Seaver, his books under one arm. Behind him stood Merric's sponsor, Faleron.

"I need help with mathematics," Seaver told Kel, his dark eyes meeting hers squarely. "Would you mind?"

Kel shook her head.

"You got space for me?" Faleron wanted to know. "I need to pick Neal's brain for this paper Sir Myles wants me to write. Besides, everybody knows it's warmer with more people in the room."

They had excuses that first time, but apparently making up fresh ones after that was too much work. Merric came with them the next night and gave no explanation at all. The newcomers became regular additions to Neal's study group. If the boys noticed that Kel left the group once an evening and came back rosy-cheeked from a run through the halls, none of them commented.

Longtime palace residents said it was the hardest winter in over a decade. Servants labored to clear paths between the outbuildings and the palace. Game grew scarce as the weeks remained cold and snows piled high. In February, Lord Wyldon and Sergeant Ezeko led the pages on an overnight hike, teaching them how to dress and camp in heavy snow. Joren picked up the tracks of a lone deer that led them to a small herd. When they took the meat to a village that had been cut off from supplies, they were welcomed gratefully.

The pages warmed up now with staffs, then moved on to sword practice. Only a day a week was spent in more complex staff work. After three weeks, Kel told Neal that she was so out of practice with pole arms that the most timid of the emperor's ladies would be able to gut her with the glaive in a flash. Neal found this infinitely amusing and told Kel that he admired her sense of humor.

Kel blinked at him. "I'm serious, Neal."

He patted her shoulder. "Of course you are."

"One day you and I will visit the Islands," she informed him, "and then you will know better."

Reviewing her schedule, Kel decided she could fit in a pattern dance before supper, and another before she went to bed. Pattern dances were linked techniques, to give the dancer practice in combat moves when no opponents were about. That night she forced herself to do a complex dance just before supper. She did a simpler one before she went to sleep. The exercises became a permanent addition to her routine.

The work she put into pattern dances and exercises for her arms began to show in practice. As her sword skills improved, Lord Wyldon and Sergeant Ezeko began to pair her with older pages. No one objected until one afternoon in late February, when Lord Wyldon was called away from the court. When he left, the older pages moved around. Kel found herself facing Zahir.

Uh-oh, she thought as the Bazhir's dark eyes blazed. I'm in trouble now.

They began with the strike-and-block combinations. Ezeko stood over them as they moved on to combinations like three high cuts, two low, with blocks to match. He watched Kel and Zahir through two complete sets and part of a third, then walked down the line to see how Quinden did against Faleron. The moment the sergeant's eyes were elsewhere, Zahir hissed, "It's time for you to take your place behind the veil, where you belong!"

He broke the drill, banging Kel's legs hard as he swung his wooden practice sword from left to right. She backed up and he followed; when he struck overhand, she knocked his sword aside and struck him in the ribs. "We don't wear veils!" she whispered in reply.

Zahir growled, "A woman out of her place is a distraction to men!" and struck her repeatedly until Kel kicked him in the stomach to make him back off. Joren, Vinson, and a few other boys closed around them to cut them off from the sergeant's view.

Neal saw them bunch up and came to Kel's defense, dragging Zahir's friends out of his way. When Vinson hit Neal from behind, the prince yanked Vinson off him. Merric threw himself onto Joren's back. Faleron and Seaver went for Zahir. The battle ended only when Sergeant Ezeko waded in and pulled everyone apart.

Lord Wyldon was livid. He sentenced all of them to a week of early-evening duty in the palace laundry. The laundrymaids, a set of rough, no-nonsense women with muscles that Kel envied, had a field day with the lads assigned to help them.

"It's not fair," Merric grumbled as he wrung out sheets. "Zahir started it."

"But you lot didn't have to pitch in," Kel

reminded him. "Besides, this may be the only time all winter that we get the mud out from under our nails."

Merric glowered at her, and Kel waited for the explosion. Instead he shook his head, smiling wryly. "Don't you get mad about *anything?*" he demanded in amused exasperation. "You know they call you the Lump."

"I try not to *show* anger," Kel explained. "The Yamanis won't talk to you if you let your feelings out. To them it's like picking your nose at table. Besides, haven't you noticed how tiring losing your temper is?"

"I've noticed it gets you punishments," the redheaded boy replied with a shrug. "Maybe it's the same thing."

"Well, you're tired at the end of both, so there you are," Kel said practically. "Help me wring out this blanket?"

⇥ nine ⇤

TESTS

*T*he week's punishment left everyone too worn out to do anything but classwork. Kel knew that was temporary. Joren, Vinson, and another third-year named Garvey had not given up their harassment of the first-years completely: during the day they took every chance to bump, casually push, or thump the younger pages. On their first night without linens to scrub, Kel changed from dress to shirt and breeches after supper, and went to Neal's room to study as usual. Merric, Seaver, the prince, Faleron, and Neal himself were there when she came in. Cleon arrived not long after she did. He sat with Neal at the writing desk, talking about a paper the third-years had to write for Master Yayin.

The room settled into its usual library-like quiet. Everyone whispered to keep from disturbing the others. Kel, Seaver, and Merric worked on the day's mathematics problems together for a while. When Kel knew that she wouldn't be needed right away, she rose and stretched. Then she casually walked out of the room.

Neal followed her and closed the door behind him. "I'd like a word," he said.

Kel looked at him. "I'll be right back," she began.

"You're not fooling me, you know," he informed her. "Every night you put on a dress for supper. That's to remind us you're a girl and you're not ashamed of it. Fine. I understand perfectly. But some nights, when you don't have punishment work and Joren and his pack are being rowdy? You go and change into your fight clothes," he waved at her shirt and breeches, "and you take a little walk. Sometimes you come back just fine, and some nights they haul you and whoever you mixed it up with before the Stump. You go looking for trouble!"

"Neal," she said nervously, "keep your voice down."

"Why? You don't seem to care if you get caught!" It was an accusation, but he lowered his voice to say it. His face turned red with the effort.

She sighed. "That's not it at all."

"Then what *is* it?" he demanded hotly. "Are you some kind of—of tavern tough that likes to brawl?"

Kel shook her head. "Not hardly, since I lose every time."

"Then what is it? I want to know!" cried Neal, his voice cracking. "I'm your friend and what you're doing worries me sick!"

"This isn't the time or the place—"

"It is if I say it is," he snapped. "I mean it, Kel. I swear by Mithros, if you try to leave I'll call the servants out myself. I'll tell the Stump." He stood between her and the halls she patrolled, arms akimbo, his green eyes mulish.

Kel ran her fingers through her hair. He really would be difficult about it; she knew him well enough to be sure of that. And she wanted someone to know she didn't get into fights because she liked it. "It's that earning-your-way custom, where the older boys make us do their errands. It's stupid and it wastes time. That's bad enough. But what Joren does, and his friends—they take it way too far. They use it to bully first-years, and that's just plain wrong."

He crossed his arms over his chest. "Oh, wonderful. You're on a hero's quest to get rid of bullies."

Kel glared at him. "Someone has to!"

"And if this wish of yours is so glorious, why haven't you asked anyone to join you, hm? We're all would-be knights, aren't we? If you aren't just enjoying the fights, why not ask for help?"

Kel planted her fists on her hips. "Because I had no reason to think I would get it!"

"What?" said a startled voice nearby.

Kel and Neal turned toward his door. At some point during their argument the boys inside had eased it open a crack to listen.

"Merric, you dolt!" they heard Faleron say. The door opened wide. They all stood there, even Prince Roald, looking at Neal and trying not to look at Kel.

"Well, she as good as said we agree with, with

Joren and his pack," stammered Merric.

Kel inspected each of them. "None of you ever spoke against it," she replied, picking her words carefully. "Even when it was you being picked on"—she rested her eyes on Seaver and Merric—"once it was over, you didn't say how it wasn't right and ought to be stopped. You just came here to Neal's room, to work with the group. I figured I was the only one here who thought it was all wrong. I thought maybe I saw it different because I'm a girl. *I* could do something about it, but I didn't think you would."

Neal turned away, running his fingers through his hair.

"Now, wait," protested Cleon. "You can't go setting tradition on its ear. Hazing is the way new boys become pages. They have to earn respect from the older ones, and we teach them to obey orders."

"So I should let this go on because it's always been that way?" she asked.

Cleon, the prince, Faleron, all nodded.

"No," she said flatly. "I know what you mean, Cleon. I do *your* chores." She met each boy's eyes. "But this custom leads to worse things. Cleon sends me for papers, but someone else traps a first-year in a corner and keeps making him do stupid tasks. He'll maybe hit the first-year to smarten him when the first-year slows down—and *that* is dead wrong. If we take this as pages, what about when we are knights? Do we say, Oh, now I'm going to be nice to the weak and the small? Or do we do as we learned when we were pages?" She stopped, breathing hard. It was the longest speech she'd ever made. "I don't mean to lecture. You can laugh and say I'm a silly girl—but when I see anyone big pick on someone small, well, there's going to be a fight." She looked at Neal. "Joren and his friends are out there looking for someone to hurt. I want to stop them."

"They'll beat you up," the prince remarked quietly.

"I think of it as combat exercise," Kel replied with grim good humor. "And I'm learning new ways to do combat all the time. So if we're all finished here?"

She walked through them and down the hall, turning into the library corridor. Running footsteps approached. She turned to find Neal.

Kel stared at him. "What do you think you're doing?"

He looked down at her for a long moment. "You're the oldest ten-year-old I've ever met," he said finally.

Exasperated, Kel put her fists on her hips. "What is *that* supposed to mean?"

Neal thrust his hands into the pockets of the breeches he wore at night. "It means I'm trying to justify to myself the fact that the best lesson I ever had on chivalry came from someone five years younger than me. When you put it that way, well, I guess I'd better help."

Kel shook her head. "All right, but it's going to hurt," she said, and set off down the hall.

"You don't have to tell me that," Neal said, keeping up with her. "Don't forget, I see your bruises every day."

They heard laughter from the stair leading to the teachers' quarters and ran to investigate. They climbed to the landing between that floor and the teachers' floor to find Joren and Vinson pushing Quinden up and down the steps as Garvey watched. The moment they saw Kel and Neal, they stopped.

Quinden made his escape. Kel, Neal, and the three senior pages, not wanting to be heard by anyone on the teachers' floor, went cautiously down the stairs. At the bottom, Joren threw a punch at Kel, who ducked. Vinson tackled Neal, who threw him into Garvey. They were in the thick of combat, giving and exchanging blows, when the air seemed to grow as heavy as velvet, weighing their limbs and shoulders down. Suddenly fighting or even speech was an effort. Slowly the five pages looked toward the stair. A tall man—a *very* tall man, Kel realized—with tousled black hair and large, dark eyes stood there, hands braced on either side of the door frame. He was dressed in a flowing white shirt and black breeches. The sparkle of magic glittered in the air between him and them.

"Such animosity will not do," he observed in a light voice. "You've managed to affect my current working; if it were to go astray...Except that it's not going to, because you are going to drop this and go do whatever it is pages are supposed to do at this time of night. Run along, please."

Although they were dismissed, none of them could move. The man frowned when he saw he wasn't being obeyed. Finally Neal managed to croak, "Spell."

"Spell? Oh, yes, of course. How careless." The sparkle of magic vanished. Kel and the others could move again. "*Now* you may go."

He turned and climbed up the stairs as Joren, Vinson, and Garvey ran. Kel and Neal remained there, staring up the stairs as the man disappeared from view around a turn.

"Will he report us?" Kel asked. If so, she wished he'd do it. She hated waiting for a summons.

Neal chuckled. "Master Numair? I doubt he'll remember why he left his workroom, once he gets back to it. That must be a sensitive spell, though, if we affected it."

"Numair," she murmured to herself with a frown. The name seemed familiar.

"Numair Salmalín," replied Neal. "Only the most powerful mage in the realm. He'll be teaching the magic classes about dragons and griffins in a month or so."

"He's Daine's—" Kel started to say "lover," but didn't when she saw Neal frown. "Friend?" she supplied hastily.

Neal sighed and nodded. "He's too old for her, you know."

Kel gave him a sympathetic pat on the back as they headed back to the others.

They were at Neal's door when he suddenly

turned cheerful. "At least Joren won't stage any of his little scrambles near the teachers' quarters again," he pointed out. "He's probably thinking right now he's lucky Master Numair didn't turn him into a tree."

"Oh, as if Master Numair could," retorted Kel. Only in stories did mages turn people into things, and she had noticed such stories always took place in the very distant past. In real life it was supposed to be impossible.

Neal grinned at her. "When he's upset enough, he can do pretty much what he wants. He turned an enemy mage into a tree just two years ago, at Fief Dunlath."

Kel gaped. "I never heard that, and we got all the news in the Islands. You're sure?"

"I had it from Father, who had it from the king."

Kel shook her head, impressed, and Neal opened his door. "Hello, my ducks," he caroled as they walked in. "Did you miss us?"

The next night, when Kel stood to go through the halls, Neal closed his book and stood with her. Faleron hesitated, then got to his feet, as did Merric. Seaver was already opening the door.

Kel looked at the other boys. Cleon had returned to study with them; his open, direct face was confused. The prince met Kel's gaze and shook his head, a wistful expression in his eyes.

Poor Roald, Kel thought. His life would be so much easier if he didn't worry about what people might say. She smiled at him and led the others outside.

There was no sign of Joren and his cronies that night, or the next. The third night they found Joren and Vinson in a courtyard, forcing Esmond of Nicoline to do bows made to a monarch over and over. The two third-years looked up, saw the size of their company, and fled. Neal slung an arm around Esmond's shoulders. "Want to join our study group?"

They had a brisk skirmish with Joren and Vinson the night after their meeting with Esmond. It ended quickly, all of them running when they heard the approach of a group of servants. The night after that, Cleon put his book aside with a sigh as Kel got up. "I'd better come keep you children out of trouble," he said with a grin at the older, taller Neal. Prince Roald and Esmond, who had joined them, stayed to work as Kel and her supporters patrolled the halls. With the addition of Cleon to their group, the fights ended. He and Neal were too big, and the others too many. Joren, Vinson, and their friends decided to find other ways to spend their time until spring.

At the end of March, another thaw was followed by a blizzard that laid more than two feet of snow on the ground. Three days later it had all melted, creating seas of mud everywhere. Planks laid on the mud to provide dry footing sank and disappeared. Weapons and unarmed combat practice were held indoors.

When they were done, Lord Wyldon demanded their attention. "I won't have good horses lamed from riding in this if it isn't necessary," he told the pages. "Instead we'll go for a run, from one end of the curtain wall to the other."

Kel's skin rippled with goose bumps. The wall that cupped the palace in a flattened half circle was thirty feet high. True, the top was broad enough to allow five men to walk abreast, but the thought of being up there made her sweat.

I should have known, she thought, trotting up a narrow stair to the top of the wall in Merric's wake. I was lucky to go for so long without facing this. I should have known it couldn't last. And I'll just have to do it, that's all.

"Waiting *bores* me!" she heard Wyldon roar from the open door above. "Get those legs moving!"

Kel locked her eyes on Merric's ankles as they ran gasping out of the tower. Don't look ahead, don't look to either side, she ordered herself. Just follow Merric.

"Go!" Wyldon bellowed. "Don't wait for permission, I told you run the wall, so *run* it. Smell that fresh air! Don't make a face, Queenscove, air is good for you. Breathe it!"

Stone after stone passed under Kel's nose. Her feet, shod in thin leather slippers, slapped the ground.

"You run like a lamb, probationer!" The boom of Wyldon's voice in her ear made her jump.

"Open your stride—put some distance between your knees. Plant those feet—don't touch on your toes and kick up your heels. I hope your precious Yamanis don't run like this."

I'd like to see how you run with a silk kimono wrapped around you from thigh to ankle, Kel thought as she lengthened her stride. The thought of Wyldon in Yamani dress made her giggle as her thigh muscles strained, then relaxed, easing into the new way to run. A quick glance ahead told Kel the boys were starting to race. Let them—she was going to stay right behind Merric's steadily churning feet.

Wyldon slowed them to a walk, then made them run again. He alternated walking and running, never allowing them to come to a complete stop. They were a strong group, hardened by a winter of short runs to the stables and back. This was an easy track, flat and dry, but the length began to tell on them. Keeping her eyes down, Kel moved up until she was between Merric and Seaver.

"How's Lord Wyldon?" she inquired, gasping.

"Fresh as rosebuds in May," growled Merric.

"Don't you two know?" Seaver asked. "His lordship runs this whole wall, both ways, every morning before dawn. My cousin says that's how he got the lungs to yell like he does."

"I hate the Stump," Merric said tightly. He liked Neal's term for Wyldon.

"As if he cares a docken," Kel remarked. "How's Neal?"

Seaver looked up, scanning the pack of older

boys. "He's ahead of everybody."

"Horse blood," guessed Merric. "There must be some in the Queenscove family."

"A racer," agreed Seaver, panting. "The family keeps it hushed up."

Kel would have laughed, but she was too breathless. She stayed with her two friends as they ran to the end of the wall. They stopped at the watchtower that marked one end of the flattened half circle.

"Keep moving!" ordered Wyldon, running in place as he watched the pages. "Don't stop—you'll cramp. If you throw up, do it outside of the wall—the wind can't blow it back in your face."

"Oh, good," gasped Esmond, who looked like he might well vomit. "That's an important tip."

I'd better not get sick, then, Kel thought. She stubbornly kept her eyes on the walkway as the boys drifted toward the view of the city. She'd heard it was splendid.

Wyldon had come to a halt. As the pages drew within earshot, he said, "You might one day command an attack on a walled fortress. How would you approach this position? Quinden of Marti's Hill?"

"I'd go around the back," he said, and smirked as the other pages laughed.

"Very true," Wyldon said frostily. "With no attacks on this palace in centuries, previous monarchs who wished to expand knocked out the rear wall. We are discussing a hypothetical, Page Quinden—a chance for you to use your imagination. How would you attack, Page Merric?"

"I'd still go around back, m'lord," replied Merric, who had caught his breath. "With the Royal Forest there, you can get men and catapults and rams really close before you're seen. Here in front, there's all that open ground between us and the Temple District."

"If you brought an army into that forest, there is a mage king in possession of the Dominion Jewel who will raise the trees and streams to fight you. He has a wildmage who would ask every vole, fox, rat, wolf, owl, and otter to harass your flanks. You would never be seen again," Wyldon informed them. "Probationer, how would you attack *this* wall? You must survey the ground before you reply."

Kel stared at Wyldon, white-faced.

Wyldon motioned for her to step up to one of the square notches between the tall stones in the wall. "Before we grow old, probationer."

Kel's legs trembled, and not just with exhaustion from the run. She forced one foot forward, then the next.

"I hope you are quicker to advise your lord in a combat situation," Wyldon told her.

Stone halted her advancing steps. She had reached the wall. Kel took a deep breath and looked out through the opening.

Straight ahead the city was a jeweled blanket on both sides of the Oloron River. It was a very pretty sight. Kel didn't feel as if she were high up, but as if she were looking at a complex tapestry.

"Our attackers have already overrun the city and put it to the torch, girl," Wyldon said overpatiently. Kel heard the other pages snickering. She was taking too long. "How must they come at us?"

It's all right, Kel thought. This isn't so bad.

Then she looked down.

Kel's ears roared; she could not catch her breath. The broad moat that passed in front of the wall was a long drop below. She heard nothing, did not feel hands prying her grip from the stone. The fear gripped her as tightly as it had on the day Conal held her over the tower balcony. Her whole body crawled with a weak, paralyzed itch.

A clean-shaven face thrust itself before hers. "Look at me, girl," a stern voice ordered. "Nowhere else. Look at my face. Whose face do you see?"

Kel blinked. That hideous drop was gone, replaced... Her eyes darted to red furrows of scar at the corner of his right eye.

"Lord Wyldon," she croaked.

"Exactly. Look at my face and turn with me." His hands on her arms tugged, twisting her body to one side. She had to move her feet or be wrapped around her own spine. She turned, her eyes locked on his.

"Now. We're on a flat place. There's stone under your feet, do you understand? Look down."

"I'll fall," she whispered.

"You can't. You're on solid ground. Just look. Curse it, girl, do as you're told!"

Instinctively—they'd all learned to jump for that tone this winter—she looked down. The only thing that she saw was stone, flat, gray, and wonderfully close.

A boy snickered. "Ooh, I'll *fall,*" someone squeaked in a falsetto voice.

Kel closed her eyes, close to tears with humiliation.

Wyldon let go of Kel. "All of you, back to the practice courts," he said. "We've time for a few rounds of staff work."

A few boys passed her, giggling. A friendly arm was slung around Kel's shoulders. "Come on, Mindelan," Neal's husky voice murmured in her ear. "We'll get you inside."

"But you're not afraid on stairs," Seaver remarked.

She cleared her throat. "Most are narrow and twisty. You can't see far in either direction. The rest of the time I just look at the next step."

"You better pray he never makes you climb Balor's Needle," Cleon advised as they entered the tower stairwell closest to the pages' wing.

"He doesn't make us run up there, does he?" Kel squeaked. Balor's Needle was the tallest part of the palace, a lean, high spire with a fragile-looking iron stair that spiraled around its length. The mages used it to observe the stars or to work spells of long-seeing that let them view the countryside around the palace and capital.

Cleon shook his head. "None of us are allowed up there. A page failed the examinations about six years ago and jumped off the Needle."

In silence they finished the walk to the court

where staff practice was held. It surprised none of them that someone might jump to his death after failing the dreaded spring examinations.

Not that *I'll* have to worry, Kel thought dully as she picked up her staff. He knows I'm afraid of heights now. He can say if I'm afraid of heights, I can't keep up with the boys, and I'll be out on my ear.

By early April Kel was able to hit the quintain's small shield every time she jousted. Her lance could only take so much of this accuracy; at last it shattered. Taking a buffet from the sandbag—she had yet to strike the small ring on the target, which would cause the bag to swing just halfway around—Kel rode Peachblossom to the quintain and dismounted, picking the pieces of her shattered lance out of the mud.

"Stop mourning like it's a dead friend," Wyldon said curtly. He'd been short with her since that day on the palace wall. "Go choose another."

Joren was ahead of her, picking a lance from the spares and holding it to Kel as she approached. Expressionless, she accepted it, knowing his eagerness to help was just so he could give her another weighted lance. This one felt no lighter than the old one. Kel ran her fingers along it and found the hair-fine breaks where plugs had been fitted back into the wood. She looked at Joren. He smirked.

Something happened to her then, something she would not be able to explain if she lived to be a thousand. A feeling like cool rain poured over her, making her feel more focused than she ever had before.

She mounted Peachblossom.

She floated in an empty space, enclosed in glass like one of Master Lindhall's animals. Outside the glass, the older boys practiced sword work from horseback as they waited their turn on the quintain, or they joked or rested, one eye on Sergeant Ezeko as he corrected Faleron's seat. A single quintain was free, the one assigned to the new pages: Esmond was next, but Lord Wyldon was showing him something as the other three first-years watched.

Unobserved, Kel kneed Peachblossom into line with the free quintain. She swung her lance into the couched position, its grip firmly in her gloved hand, the butt passed snugly between her ribs and arm. The long, tapered end thrust out over the gelding's withers at just the right angle to hit the shield. Gently she kicked Peachblossom, urging him forward at a trot. Her world narrowed to one small, painted circle on a slab of wood. She was halfway down the lane, and everything—her seat, her grip, the heft of the lance—felt perfect in a way it never had before.

"Charge," she whispered to Peachblossom. She hadn't demanded that speed from him since their first try at the quintain.

He lowered his head and charged, hooves thundering on the damp, springtime ground.

Kel rose to meet the target, her lance aimed at the circle. She struck it dead center. The target snapped to the side, precisely as it did for the third- and fourth-year pages, the quintain turning neatly. Kel galloped past, waiting for the bruising impact of the sandbag. It never came.

She raised her lance and drew back on the reins, guiding Peachblossom into a gentle turn. She was almost certain that the gelding congratulated her. "Extra oats for you tonight," she murmured, slowing him to a walk.

Wyldon watched her, arms crossed over his chest. "Good," he said. "When you can do it reliably, instead of once or twice, you will have something."

Kel didn't hesitate. She knew the feel of it now. She walked Peachblossom into a turn and pointed him at the target. One of the pages had already set it for the next tilter. Kel tucked her lance butt under her arm, lowered it until it crossed the gelding's shoulders, and urged him into a trot, then a gallop, then the charge. Everything that had been so perfect a few moments ago felt exactly right again. She struck the circle dead center a second time, then went back and did it a third time and a fourth. After her fifth perfect tilt, she stopped in front of Lord Wyldon.

"Very good, probationer." Wyldon sounded as if his teeth hurt to say it. The other pages had all stopped what they were doing to watch her last three passes. "You are released for the remainder of the morning."

She bowed to him from the saddle and turned Peachblossom toward the stables.

The sound of applause made her turn in the saddle. "Huzzah, Kel!" Neal cried gleefully. "Huzzah, huzzah!" The prince, Merric, Seaver, Faleron, and Cleon were all clapping and cheering. So were Eda Bell, the Shang Wildcat, and Stefan the hostler, who often came to watch the tilting practice. She waved to them with a grin, and nudged Peachblossom to a trot.

The examinations at the end of April had existed for only fourteen years. King Jonathan's father had introduced them after the discovery that a girl— Alanna the Lioness—had concealed her sex to become a knight. The suspicion that trickery was involved had led King Roald to create public tests.

Now anyone could watch as a panel of nobles, mages, and teachers asked pages questions about their classwork and watched them show their physical skills in practice bouts of all kinds. Only three boys had failed the examinations since they were set up, yet all the pages were convinced that they would be the next. Even the prospect of the lesser examinations, the "little tests," which gave younger pages experience in public questions and performance, made them nervous.

Kel dreaded the public exams, but she was beginning to think that this year's tests would be the only ones she would get to take. Lord Wyldon would never let her return in the fall. He was as cold to her in April as he'd been in September. He still referred to her as "probationer," which seemed like a bad sign.

Knowing that, she had to force herself to study for the little tests. The reality was an anticlimax: their audience was tiny, the classroom questions basic. The pages had to write and do mathematical problems on a large slate so everyone watching could follow their work. They had to recite the Code of Ten, the set of laws that formed the basis of government in most realms north of the Inland Sea. They reported aloud on the habits and behavior of some species of immortal—Kel chose hurroks. Then they demonstrated three different ways to greet dignitaries. That marked the end of the classroom work.

Going to the outdoor practice court for their examinations, the first-year pages had to saddle, mount, and ride their horses around a ring. They went through the most basic maneuvers with unarmed combat, staff, wooden practice sword, and bow. Then, to Kel's surprise and relief, it was over. All of the first-years passed.

"I keep telling you, these tests have to be easy enough that even a noble with ogre blood could pass," Neal informed her at supper that night.

Kel grinned, but said, "You know, ogres only sound stupid. Most are pretty smart."

"And it's a shallow person who judges anyone by the way they sound," he admitted cheerfully. "I'm so shallow I'm surprised I don't reflect myself."

Kel groaned and punched him in the shoulder. The next week Kel, Neal, and the other pages watched the big tests, in which the fourth-year pages were publicly quizzed and made to demonstrate their mastery of the skills they would need as squires. Kel was surprised that neither Lord Raoul—the Knight Commander of the King's Own—nor Alanna the Lioness as King's Champion was among the judges, and mentioned it to Neal.

"Well, of course *they* can't decide on whether or not a page is suitable," Neal replied. "None of the knights from that generation are allowed to judge. Quite a few of our stuffier nobles claim the pages and squires in those years collaborated to get the Lioness made a knight, though of course no one says as much to their faces. Even Duke Gareth the Elder—her training master—has never served. The king picked the oldest, blue-bloodedest, fustiest men in the realm to do the tests, ones who were nowhere near the palace for Lady Alanna's training. That keeps the traditionalists happy so His Majesty can then get them to go along with things like opening schools on their estates."

"How *dare* they say the Lioness cheated!" growled Kel. "Great Goddess, she fights ogres and spidrens and *armies* all the time—"

"You really look up to her, don't you?" Neal asked.

"She's a hero. She's proved it over and over."

"And will go on doing so until the day she dies," he said evenly. "You can smack some people in the face with a haddock and they'll still call it a mouse if a mouse is what they want to see. She's

learned to live with that. Perhaps you should, too."
After a pause, he asked, "Have you ever met her?"

"We were away, and now—she's had a busy
year," whispered Kel, hanging her head. "So busy
she hasn't even visited Their Majesties."

He seemed about to say something, but he
changed his mind. "I want to hear this," he said as
the judges quizzed a page on the law regarding
illegal settlement.

That night in the mess hall, the fourth-year
pages moved to the half of the room where the
squires sat. Everyone applauded. There was cake
for dessert and a juggler, a special treat from Lord
Wyldon for the new squires.

It marked the beginning of a lazy May.
Throughout the month knights drifted in and out
of the practice courts, looking at the new squires.
Only simple reading assignments were given in
afternoon classes. There was no etiquette class:
Master Oakbridge was in charge of arranging the
monarchs' summer travels throughout the realm,
and had not a moment to spare. Only in the practice courts was the pages' schedule the same.

With the arrival of warmer weather Kel's sparrows had moved back into the courtyard. In May
the babies began to explore the world outside their
nests. Kel loved to watch the tiny birds. They
approached their parents or Kel with wings aflut-
ter, yellow-rimmed beaks wide open, cheeping
plaintively until they were fed. When not hungry,
they seemed to view the world with the gravity of
aged priests, watching everything around them

with great earnestness. Crown's fledglings were every bit as alert as their mother, reaching their seed before all of the other youngsters. They were also the first to shed their baby feathers; Kel was able to recognize them only when they begged their mother for extra food.

At the beginning of June, the pages began to prepare for their weeks in camp. They were issued summer clothes much like their practice garments, and taught how to load a packhorse with supplies and gear. Their first class of the day for a week was neither reading nor writing, but the art of calculating the amount of supplies necessary to keep four adults—Lord Wyldon, Sergeant Ezeko, the Shang Horse, and the Shang Wildcat—and twenty-odd pages for two months.

Finally Lord Wyldon gave them an entire day to run last-minute errands and laze. They were to leave for the depths of the Royal Forest in the morning, after breakfast.

The next morning Kel rose at her usual early time. She gave her sparrows one last feeding. "You stay out of trouble," she ordered them as they pecked at their seed. Salma was to look after them while she was gone. Kel refused to think of who would care for them in the fall. Lord Wyldon had still not given any sign that she might be allowed to return.

Overhead, the great bell clanged, summoning those who were late risers from their beds. Gathering her saddlebags, Kel left her room.

ten

THE ROYAL FOREST

*T*he morning's ride into the Royal Forest seemed more like a picnic expedition than training. The pages were silly and giddy. They snatched at leaves, pushing at each other and telling jokes. Riding at the front of their column with Hakuin, Wyldon ignored them. Kel was at the end of the line, because Peachblossom tolerated another horse and rider near him for just so long. Neal, Merric, Prince Roald, and Eda would keep her company for a time, then move off to give the big gelding the solitude he clearly desired.

Kel noticed clouds gathering before lunch. Few of the boys had. They were shocked when it began to pour in mid-afternoon. "It's not like the rain's a surprise," Kel murmured to her mount. "And it's not like they aren't used to mud." She preferred being wet to being muddy, though she knew she wouldn't feel that way after dark, when it got cold.

They followed a broad, well-traveled track most of the day. Wyldon halted the column when they reached a wide clearing with an immense ancient oak at its center. Most of the riders led their mounts under the tree's scant protection, while four of the oldest pages went to search for water and cover. It was a test of their hunt skills, as well as Lord Wyldon's way of letting them know that they were now senior pages, expected to master the hardest chores.

Two returned quickly, having found a stream and shallow caves on the ground above it. Wyldon showed the first-years how to leave a trail sign that would tell the two pages who had not yet returned the path they had taken. Kel got hers right on the second try, but Seaver and Quinden had yet to put the stones and twigs in the correct formation when the missing pages returned. Finally Quinden got it, but Wyldon kept them all until Seaver laid the sign correctly.

Kel waited for the others to lead their horses into the open ground past her before she brought Peachblossom out. "Don't feel bad," she murmured to Seaver as he trudged by. "Next time, picture it in your mind like it's a drawing of a building, or a map. That's how I do it."

"It just wasn't making sense," he whispered to her.

"That's why making it a picture helps. That gives it sense."

Seaver gripped her shoulder in wordless thanks, keeping an eye on Peachblossom.

A short thunderstorm rolled in as they set up camp. Chilly air followed; Kel felt it even before she finished rubbing Peachblossom down. Once she'd fed him and eaten, she wrapped herself in a blanket and closed her eyes. Breathing slowly and softly, as she'd been taught, she made herself believe that she was comfortable as she drifted off to sleep.

Wyldon roused them at dawn. It rained steadily as they ate lumpy porridge made by Cleon, saddled their horses, and rode out. They followed the stream southeast, fording it often to skirt boggy ground. When the rainfall got heavier, Lord Wyldon guided them onto higher ground, lecturing them on the dangers of flash floods.

On they rode in the rain. The grumbling started when Lord Wyldon had them mount up after a short lunch break. The boys continued to complain as they followed a path up into rocky ground. Kel was downwind of Vinson when she heard him growl, "This *isn't* necessary. It's not like we're on a mission. Why can't we find a village to hole up in until this stops?"

"A village?" Kel heard a chill voice inquire. "Do I take it you would like to change our arrangements, Page Vinson?"

Kel shook her head. Vinson still hadn't learned that Lord Wyldon often turned up where he was least wanted.

At least he knew when it was bad to lie. "Yes, my lord," Vinson said nervously. "There's no need to be out in this. We should find someplace dry and wait till it clears."

"I see. And you, Joren? Cleon?"

"Our mounts would like the change, my lord,"

Kel heard Cleon reply. From his tone, he knew Wyldon probably would not listen. "So would I."

"We don't need to be pushing on like this, m'lord," added Joren.

Kel listened in wonder. The emperor would have taken the heads of any warrior who questioned his orders.

As Peachblossom trudged around the next bend in the trail, Kel saw Lord Wyldon. He stood on the grass at the side of the path. "Well, girl?" he inquired. "I suppose you would like a nice warm place to sit, like the others?"

"What I like doesn't matter, Lord Wyldon," she replied steadily. "It's what you want." That didn't sound right. She brushed her dripping hair back. "I didn't mean it the way it came out."

After a pause he asked, "How did you mean it?"

"You're the warrior in charge," she explained. "In battle you could hit me or put me in irons if I questioned you. Why should you let me do it now? Enemies could be out to jump us right here, and you wouldn't hear them because you'd be talking to me."

Someone chuckled: Hakuin, the Shang Horse. He'd been riding with the pack animals since lunch and had now come up behind Kel. "Whatever you think of us Yamanis, Lord Wyldon, we know how to train even young warriors. Though I expected no less from Ilane of Mindelan's daughter," he told Kel, and bowed.

She bowed in reply. It was easy to accept a

compliment to her mother.

"What has her mother to do with anything?" Wyldon asked tiredly.

"You don't know?" asked the Shang warrior. "It's the reason our emperor agreed to a treaty and marriage with Tortall. Five years ago Ilane of Mindelan caught Scanran pirates stealing our most sacred objects. She rescued the Gods' Swords and protected them from recapture until the Imperial Guard arrived. I believe that Keladry was there, were you not?"

Kel nodded. After that fight, the emperor had welcomed her entire family into his inner circle, on the same level as the greatest families of his realm.

"You have much in common with Lady Ilane, my lord," said Hakuin with a needling smile.

"What weapons did she have?" Wyldon asked, after a moment.

"A glaive, my lord," Kel replied in a low voice.

Wyldon grunted. He swung into his saddle and rode up the trail.

Hakuin smiled at Kel. "Nice of you to let your friends ride pillion." He winked, and rode away.

Her friends? Kel twisted to look behind her. Sparrows clung to her bedroll and saddlebags. They came and went rapidly, so they were hard to count, but she decided that ten or eleven of them were on Peachblossom or in the air. "Bright Mithros," she breathed. "Don't tell me food is so short that you thought you *had* to follow me."

One female peeped at her and fluttered around to perch on the front of Kel's saddle. It was

Crown. "The pickings are going to be very lean," Kel warned.

Crown peeped again and turned so she could watch the road ahead.

Kel heard the training master at the head of their group. "We stop when I say stop, and batten on a village when I say to!" he called, his voice clear even in the rain. "If you're riding in answer to a call for help, you can't pick your weather—and what if that village is low on food? Do I saddle them with your appetites *and* those of your mounts? Knights provide for themselves on the road. If the village has extra food you pay for it, but I'll tell you right now, at this time of year, many have no surplus. Use your heads—and keep riding!"

It was even colder than it had been the night before. Everything was soaked. To Kel's surprise, Lord Wyldon allowed Prince Roald to use his magic to start two large fires. Perhaps his lordship decided we were practical enough today, and he would like to be warm, she thought.

She fed her sparrows some of the trail bread that had been with the packhorses. At least the general supplies had been packed in oiled cloth to shed the wet. Everyone hung their blankets near the fires to dry. The cloth was still damp but warm as the weary riders wrapped the blankets around their bodies and went to sleep.

To everyone's relief, the next day dawned bright and clear. The group set out after breakfasting on lumpy porridge. It was not quite noon when they entered a broad clearing, startling a herd of deer into flight. There stood a long house built of logs with a rough stable behind it.

"Home for the next two months," Lord Wyldon said. "Stable your mounts, care for them properly, then assemble with your packs."

Once they had gathered in front of the house, Wyldon took them inside. It was a shed more than a house. There were two hearths and no chairs, benches, tables, or beds. They could sleep on the floor or in the clearing outside, Lord Wyldon told them. There were chores to be done: the chimneys inspected and cleared, a winter's accumulation of trash to be swept out. Pages were delegated to fetch water and gather firewood from the forest floor. Sergeant Ezeko showed the first-years how to dig latrines, then ordered Quinden and Seaver to set one up for the boys. Once they had gone, the sergeant turned to Keladry.

"Find a protected spot on the opposite side of camp from the boys' latrine, and dig one for use by you and the Shang Wildcat," he ordered. "Also, you are to sleep where she does. If she wants to sleep outdoors, that is what you do. Do I make myself clear?"

Kel nodded. "Yes, sir."

Ezeko gave her a shovel. "Dig well away from the stream."

Kel scouted for a good spot in a clump of bushes and dug a trench as the sergeant had instructed. Once she was done, she found Eda Bell and showed her the latrine. In her turn, Eda showed her where she'd already hung a hammock between two sturdy trees. The Wildcat offered Kel the use of a spare hammock, but Kel preferred to sleep on the ground. A grassy patch close by would make her bedroll as soft as a mattress. Together they stretched a piece of canvas over the area to keep off the wet.

Lunch came next: cold meat, trail bread, and dried fruit. Lord Wyldon told the pages they might do as they wished for a while, provided they didn't stray too far from the house. He settled for a long talk with the Shang warriors and Ezeko. Quite a few boys, including Neal, decided to take a nap. Kel was considering a nap of her own, but decided that she needed to try out her latrine first. She headed back to her clump of bushes.

She was just finishing when she heard footsteps in the brush and giggles. Curse those boys! she thought, trying to pull her loincloth and breeches up.

They were coming nearer. Her clothes tangled, and she nearly fell.

Suddenly the bushes erupted in a flurry of whistles and angry bird chatter. One of the boys yelped; another cried, "Where'd these birds come from?!" She heard the boys stumble and crash as they ran, followed by a storm of irate sparrows.

Kel laughed until she cried. Fixing her clothes, she left her latrine. Her sparrows swirled around her, then settled into a bush. From the way they peeped and cheeped at one another, it was clear they were pleased with themselves.

On her way back to camp, Kel was about to pass a thick-boled tree when she heard the rasp of cloth on bark. It was enough warning. When Joren lunged at her, wrapping an arm around her throat, she was ready. She slid from his grasp, bringing him up and over her back in a combination twist and pull. Straight into a holly bush he went. It was a throw she had learned in the Islands, not one they'd been taught by the two Shangs.

You'd think he'd've seen by now I have a few tricks to me, she thought as he thrashed in the holly. The sparrows, hearing the noise, came racing to Kel. They darted at Joren in single attacks, screeching in fury.

"Stop it," Kel told them. "Let the bush peck him." To her surprise the birds obeyed. Kel watched Joren for a few moments, thinking. Finally she walked over to him. "You do no credit to Lord Wyldon mucking about like this," she said, keeping her face Yamani-smooth and emotionless.

He reached for her with a snarl. Kel stepped back. He was none too pretty now. His fair skin was scratched by sparrow and holly, his flaxen hair a rat's nest, and rage twisted his face.

"He'll prize anyone who rids him of you," Joren snapped, fighting the bush to get at her.

"He said that?" she asked.

"He doesn't need to. Anyone can see it," Joren told her, his voice filled with venom. "You're going to regret you ever set foot in the palace."

"You'll have to get out of that bush first," Kel

pointed out coolly, and walked away. When she reached camp, she saw that Quinden and Garvey sported facial scrapes and peck marks. "Nasty scratches," she remarked. "You should have them looked at." Quinden at least had the shame to look away.

She left them to curry Peachblossom and do some hard thinking. Was Joren right? Did Lord Wyldon want to be rid of her so badly? If that were the case, perhaps she ought to quit now, and go home.

That made her pause in her grooming. Peachblossom looked at her; when she did not instantly resume work, he gently clamped his jaws around her forearm.

Kel nodded grimly. Peachblossom was right: she had to hang on. She had to fight even harder. There was still time to convince everyone that she belonged here.

"Everyone, assemble," Wyldon called as she was putting her brushes away. "Time to get to work."

Once he'd gathered the pages, he assigned them to groups. There were at least one third-year page and one of the first-years in each. The older pages were to start teaching the new ones how to create maps; the two Shang warriors and Sergeant Ezeko would roam, checking on them.

Wyldon sent all but one of the groups from the clearing to map different pockets of ground, on the other side of the ridge that sheltered the clearing in the west and south, or on the other side of the broad stream that bordered the clearing in the north and east. The remaining group included Kel, Neal, and Cleon.

"You're going to find a vantage point that overlooks this clearing," Wyldon told them. "You'll map the area, including prominent features such as rock formations and the stream. Once you come down you will pace the dimensions between features and mark them on your map. Cleon's done it before." Lord Wyldon pointed to a nearby chestnut, one that grew on the clearing's edge near the stream. "Start climbing," he ordered.

The two boys scrambled up with ease, finding plenty of hand and toe holds. Kel stared at the tree, shaking.

"I issued an order," Lord Wyldon said quietly. "That tree will grow no shorter."

Maybe he won't get rid of me because I'm afraid of heights! Kel thought. It had been her fear ever since that first run on the palace wall. He's giving me a chance to handle it. So if I want to convince him I deserve to stay, this is where it starts.

She made herself walk to the tree and put her hands on it. It was solid, reassuring: an old tree. Where the trunk sank into the earth, the roots were mounded, giving her a step up. She rested her foot against one knob, making sure her foot would not slip, then lunged up to grab the first low-hanging branch that would take her weight. Eyes shut tight, she mounted that branch as she would Peachblossom and straddled it, facing the trunk.

She rested her forehead against its bark and felt around for the next-highest branch.

"Keladry?" whispered Cleon from somewhere high above. "Neal, is she coming?"

"You boys start mapping!" ordered Lord Wyldon.

This isn't so bad, Kel told herself, though she shook so hard that her teeth clicked together. Opening her eyes a hair, she glanced up and saw the next branch.

"What is the next step, probationer?" demanded Wyldon.

"Stand," she whispered. She must, if she wanted to grab the upper branch.

"Then do so."

Kel took a breath, shut her eyes once more, and clutched the trunk. Wobbling, she got one foot under her and pushed up. She slid her palms higher, jamming her fingertips into her target. Wrapping her arms around it in a death grip, she pulled herself into a standing position.

"Mount up," ordered the calm voice below. It steadied her. Without opening her eyes, Kel tightened her grip on the higher branch and swung herself onto it, again as if she mounted a bareback Peachblossom.

"Next branch," ordered Lord Wyldon. "You're nowhere near the top."

"I knew that," whispered Kel to herself. "I did."

She heard a rustle and a soft cheeping sound. Crown lit on a twig near her face, peering at Kel as if worried. A series of light impacts told Kel the rest of the small flock had landed on her shoulders and clothes.

"Shoo," whispered the girl. "You can't help, though I'm glad that you'd want to."

"Are you praying up there, probationer?" demanded Wyldon from below.

"Please shoo," Kel told the birds. "Go see Neal. He'd like some company, I bet."

The flock took off, leaving Crown behind. A moment later Kel heard Neal cry, "Where did these birds come from? They—that tickles!" and Cleon's startled laugh.

Looking up to see the boys, she saw the next large branch instead. If I stand, she thought, I can swing myself onto that branch like I did this one.

"I think I have it now," she told Crown. Looking up was easy. She could at least see where she wanted to go.

Kel refused to think about how she was going to climb down.

She inched forward until she could hold on to the trunk. Bracing herself, she stood. One foot slipped. Instinctively she opened her eyes to place it better.

The ground on one side of the chestnut fell away sharply. Fifteen feet below her position lay the stream that ran along the clearing's edge. The water, studded with rocks, swayed before her eyes. Her ears rang. Terror swamped her. She wrapped her arms around her branch and froze as Crown chattered in alarm.

In the end, Neal and Cleon had to climb down to help her out of the tree. When at last Kel stood before Lord Wyldon, he told her, "You have to disarm your fear, or it will make a cripple of you."

Kel nodded, miserably. Was there a polite way to say that she was about to be sick?

"You will climb this tree every day. If we cannot cure you of fear, you must learn to work despite it, understand?" Wyldon eyed her, then added, "If you must vomit, bury it when you are done. A knight hides all sign of his presence as much as he can."

Kel nodded and went behind a bush. When she was done, he ordered the three of them to start mapping the clearing on foot.

As always, the training master was as good as his word. Each day, in addition to working with her teachers and Peachblossom, he sent her into the chestnut tree. There was no set time for the exercise: he might order her to do it first thing in the morning or even after dark, to report on the animals she heard. Sometimes the boys were off doing other tasks; often they were not. Kel learned to ignore their jokes and listen only for Lord Wyldon's orders. He always watched when he sent her into the tree. So did the sparrows, unless it was after dark.

"I'll never be able to eat chestnuts again," the girl told Neal after a few weeks of climbing. While she had thrown up less as the weeks passed, it still happened. That day a high wind tossed the branches, making her slip repeatedly. Once she was safe on the ground, she brought up what felt like a hundred meals. A fine way to celebrate my birthday, she thought as she buried the mess under leaves. She had remembered that she turned eleven that day as she clung to a swaying branch.

"This is sheer torture," Neal snapped. "He's trying to make you quit. That way no one can say he got rid of you even though you do as well as the rest of us."

It was strange to hear Neal voice the same thoughts as Joren. "He's teaching me to work through it," she said, rinsing her mouth with a handful of cold water. She had to do it twice: the first time she had trembled so badly that most of the water spilled from her palm. "I climbed twenty-three feet today."

"With all of the pages watching and making jokes and betting on where you'll freeze up? He's trying to make you quit," insisted Neal.

Kel looked up at him and sighed. "And I'm not going to let him."

"You don't have a choice. He hates you," Neal told her, exasperated. "The king forced you on him. He made sure the Lioness couldn't even go near you—"

Kel stared at him, not sure that she'd heard correctly. "The Lioness what?"

Neal sighed. "She told Father. Lord Wyldon got the king to order her to stay completely away from you. He said it would be favoritism, since she's never shown an interest in the pages before.

He even suggested Lady Alanna might—you know"—Neal twiddled his fingers to suggest magic—"to help you."

It was suddenly hard for Kel to breathe. "You mean—she doesn't hate me? She isn't staying away because, because—I don't know. Because she wants to be the only lady knight?"

"It's hard to say how she feels about you, since you've never met," Neal pointed out wryly. "But Father says she's never been so angry with the king for so long."

"I guess it *would* seem like she played favorites," Kel remarked slowly. "That wouldn't be fair. But why did he put me on probation if he meant to be fair to me?"

Neal looked at her soberly. "Aren't you begging the question?"

Kel blinked at him. "Can't you ever ask something right out, instead of walking all around it?"

"Begging the question means you state or assume something that hasn't been proved. In this case, you're assuming the Stump can actually think."

"That's not very useful, Neal," Kel said impatiently.

"If I were useful, you wouldn't know it was me," he replied loftily. In a quieter tone he said, "Anyway, now you know why you haven't seen the Lioness." He patted her shoulder awkwardly and wandered off. Kel found a rock and sat, resting her chin on her knees. She had a great deal to think about.

*   *   *

Early one morning at the end of June, Eda Bell
roused Kel from a sound sleep. "What time is it?"
the girl mumbled, grabbing her breeches and
struggling into them.

"Not quite dawn." The Wildcat rolled up her
hammock with the quickness of long practice.
"Lord Raoul and thirty of the King's Own rode in
not too long ago. Some village has a very bad spidren problem. We're all going to hunt them
down." She passed Kel a small cup of green tea.

"What's 'very bad'?" Kel asked between sips.
Her head was clearing.

"The villagers report five, maybe ten of the
things. Maybe more. They took a woman and
some livestock."

Kel got to her knees, and folded her bedroll as
quickly as her fingers could work.

⇥ eleven ⇤

SPIDREN HUNT

*A*fter a hard morning's ride, they were given shelter from the light rain in the forest village's largest barn. Once the horses were tended, everyone gathered around the Knight Commander to eat. At first there was no sound but chewing; they were so hungry that even oatcakes, dried fruit, and water tasted good.

Finally Lord Raoul cleared his throat. "You young fellows may not know, but rain is good for this kind of work. We can track better in the mud—and with spidrens, we need all the help we can get. We can't use dogs this time. Unless they're trained for it, dogs won't hunt 'em—they just turn tail and run. Maybe they're smarter than we are."

There was a quiet chuckle from his listeners.

"We have talismans to warn us of their presence, but the spidrens have spells to shield themselves. They're absolutely fearless, too. You first- and second-year pages, you'll carry staffs. If you're attacked, use the staff to hold the beast off and yell like mad. I mean it. No heroics."

"Not against spidrens," commented a blunt-nosed Bazhir. "They'll gag you in web and hack your arms off before you know your sword is gone."

"Spidrens will stick to the trees if they're thick, as they are hereabouts," continued the Knight Commander. "That's what they prefer. They also go for bare rock. That's why they're hard to track. Now, will one of you local fellows give us a map?"

A young man in a hunter's greens and browns came forward. He used a stick to draw in the beaten earth of the floor, marking out streams, hills, and gorges. Everyone paid close attention.

At last Lord Raoul got to his feet. There was a lot of him to straighten from a crouch. Seen from close by, his shoulders and chest were as broad as the palace wall. "We hunt spidrens *together*," he said. "No going off alone because you think you see something. Each of you pairs with one of my men. Tell *him* if you see anything of interest. Now, arm up."

"Horses?" asked one of the third-year pages.

"You heard our guide. A lot of what's around is boggy. You don't want spidrens above you when your mount is wallowing. The horses stay here," replied Lord Raoul.

"I'm just as glad," Kel told Peachblossom, slipping him an apple. "I'd hate to risk you on something when I don't know what I'm about." Peachblossom slobbered on her tunic, as if he bestowed a horse's blessing.

Lord Raoul's second in command, Captain Flyndan, paired up men and pages briskly. Kel was placed in the charge of the older Bazhir soldier, the one who had mentioned arms getting hacked off. He nodded to her. "I am Qasim," he said, and pointed to her shoulders. "You have a feather rash."

She blinked, confused, then realized what he was talking about. The sparrows were so light she forgot they perched on her. "Sorry, sir," she said meekly. "I don't have much control over them. Once we're moving, they'll go into the trees."

To her surprise the hard-faced man offered an open hand to her friends. He had grain in his palm. The grin on his face as the small birds lit on his palm and helped themselves made Kel smile in reply. When the grain was eaten and the sparrows returned to Kel, he was all business again. "Get your staff—what's your name?" The second in command had made his pairings by pointing to page, then soldier.

"Kel, sir."

"I am only Qasim, not 'sir.' Get your staff."

Kel obeyed. As she did, she noticed that the third- and fourth-year pages were armed with long spears, as were half of the men of the Own. The remaining men bore crossbows. All of the soldiers and the third- and fourth-year boys carried swords as well.

I wish I had a *glaive*, Kel thought passionately. She was scared. If only Lord Wyldon weren't so fixed in his ways!

Once they were armed, Lord Raoul broke them into three groups, ten soldiers in each. He led one group. Captain Flyndan had the group including Kel and Qasim, while Lord Wyldon took the third. One of the village men was placed with each group as a guide. Neal was in Lord Raoul's group. Kel was a little jealous; she would have liked to watch the famed knight's work at close range.

They communicated by means of spelled pendants worn by each group leader. Qasim explained the advantage of the pendants: the spidrens wouldn't realize they had been seen, since they wouldn't hear a horn call. They would have less chance to summon help. The men of the King's Own also used a secret language of hand signals while they were in sight of one another.

As their company moved into the surrounding forest, the rain continued to fall. It deadened the sounds of their passage. That quiet was comforting to Kel. There was a difference between coming up behind grazing deer and approaching a prey that was clever, vicious, large, and fast. The thought of being stone was not helpful just then. She remembered her mother, facing the Scanran raiders. Had the Lioness, in battle against giants, felt as if she wanted to crawl away to someplace safe? Of course not—and neither would Kel. She would be steadfast, like her mother. Like Alanna the Lioness.

The hunters followed the signs left when the spidrens had taken a cow, which was too big to be carried through the trees. When that trail ended at a stream, the three companies split up. Halts were called as each group found something that might lead them to their foes. All those clues to the spidrens' whereabouts failed. The creatures knew they would be hunted. They were careful to hide their tracks.

Now and then someone would find abandoned webs. The men of the King's Own could judge from experience just how old the things were and how long it had been since spidrens had used them.

It was nervous work. All of them, even the veteran men, kept one eye on the trees. This part of the forest was old and untouched by humans; some trees rose over one hundred and thirty feet into the air. Kel saw how they would make a road for creatures that could swing across gaps on web ropes. On the forest floor the light was gray, weaving through the foliage to brush carpets of rotting brown leaves. While the tree cover held the worst of the rain off the hunters, it dripped dully, adding to the gloomy feel of the air. They heard no animals except Kel's sparrows, who chattered and talked among themselves.

After yet another halt as they waited to see if someone else had found anything useful, Qasim sat on a log and nodded for Kel to do the same. Half of the sparrows climbed on the man to see if he'd hidden more seed from them. The rest sat on or beside Kel, fluffing wet feathers and shaking themselves out. Crown hopped onto Kel's knee and eyed her, head tilted first to one side.

Kel offered a finger. When Crown hopped on, she raised the bird before her face. "I wish I were

Daine," she said very quietly. "I'd ask if you could flit about and find these spidrens. You'd be wonderful spies."

"We shall find them. We must," Qasim assured her. When Kel raised her eyebrows in question, he explained, "Often they bite off a victim's limb, then slap web on it, to keep them from dying of blood loss. The woman they took may yet live."

Kel felt her stomach roll. "I *really* wish we could find them, then," she said hotly. "And sooner rather than later. They *are* monsters."

Captain Flyndan waved them to their feet. Word had come through: another dead end. As Kel stood, Crown hopped to the log and began to chatter. When she stopped, the entire flock sped off. Kel shrugged and resettled her grip on her staff.

They searched through boggy ground that threatened to yank their boots from their feet, then uphill until they rejoined Lord Raoul's and Lord Wyldon's groups. As the men and pages relaxed, the officers went apart to confer. Kel was having a drink from her water bottle when the sparrows returned, twittering and shrieking. They whirled around her like a small cyclone.

Neal, who had come over to talk with her, covered his ears with muddy hands. "Must they be so shrill?" he demanded.

Crown and a male sparrow hovered before Kel's face. They both clutched a long stick. When Kel held out her hands, the sparrows dropped their burden. Holding up the stick, Kel noticed a fat, gray-green worm was dangling from the end. Or was it a worm? She looked closer. She had seen this gray-green stuff before.

"Qasim?"

He snatched the twig from her hands. "My lord," he called. Grabbing Kel's shoulder, Qasim towed her over to Lord Raoul, Lord Wyldon, and Captain Flyndan. Kel's sparrows trailed her like a flying scarf, with Neal close behind them. Crown perched on the girl's shoulder and wiped her beak on Kel's ear.

Qasim gave the twig to Lord Raoul. The big man raised his eyebrows and touched the web. It clung so well that he had to use his belt-knife to scrape it off his skin. "This is fresh," he commented, letting Lord Wyldon have a look at it. "Where did you find this?"

Qasim pointed to Kel, who gulped. "My lord—" she began.

"Call him 'sir'—he prefers it," murmured Qasim.

"Sir," Kel said, "my sparrows brought it to me."

"Pets?" asked Lord Raoul, raising his brows. "We weren't allowed them in my day."

"They aren't pets, exactly," Kel explained nervously, keeping an eye on Lord Wyldon. "They live in the courtyard outside my room, and I feed them, and—they seem to like me. And Neal—Neal of Queenscove—he says palace animals are so much cleverer since Daine came there..." Lord Wyldon's mouth twisted, and Kel shut up.

"Too bad they can't lead us to the spidrens," Lord Raoul remarked with a sigh. "Any idea on how far they might have flown before they encountered this?"

Kel shook her head. She had an idea, though she knew Lord Wyldon would not want to hear it. She hesitated, then decided she had nothing to lose. "My lord knight commander," she began.

Qasim nudged her.

"Sir," Kel corrected herself. "I think they could lead us to the spidrens."

"Are you a wildmage too?" asked the big knight. "You can speak with them?"

"No," Kel admitted, "but I think they understand more than you'd guess."

"They know who's planning a dirty trick on Kel and who isn't," Neal said abruptly. "They know who's her friend and who isn't."

"Sir, if Kel thinks they might lead us, maybe we should listen." Kel looked around, startled. Faleron had drawn closer while Sir Raoul had examined the spidren web.

"She's smart about a lot of things," added Merric, standing close to Neal. "Whatever *some* people say." Neal and Faleron nodded agreement when Lord Raoul looked at each of them.

Crown rose from her shoulder, fluttering, and called to the others. They flew with her to the clearing's edge and perched on a tree. Crown then flew back to Kel, chattering, turned, and rejoined her flock.

Lord Raoul scratched his head. "This is what

I've come to," he said mournfully. "Following little birdies." He singled out first a local guide, then ten pages and soldiers, including Qasim and Joren. To his second he said, "I'll take 'em, Flyndan. You might want to break out blazebalm and torches." He glanced at the sky. "It'll be dark soon. Feed everyone, and save some for us. All right, young-ster," he told Kel, "they know you best, and your friends seem to think you've a head on your shoul-ders. Let's see how quiet you can lead. You're on point."

"But, sir—" she argued. Wyldon would never approve.

"They're your birds," Sir Raoul told her. "Do you think they can lead us? If you're not sure, we'll just keep fumbling around."

Crown cheeped impatiently at Kel. The girl took a deep breath. "Yes, sir, I think they can lead us."

"Then let's go," ordered Sir Raoul.

Kel looked up into the big man's sloe-black eyes and sighed. Resettling her grip on her staff, she walked over to the sparrows' tree. They took off, leading her toward a trail through a cut in two rocks. She advanced as quietly as she knew how, keeping an eye for brush and pebbles underfoot. She was on her mettle with seven men and three of the pages following. Even if I can't come back, she thought fiercely, I'll have done this much. I'll have led a spidren hunting party.

The sparrows landed within view, on top of a flat rock. As soon as she drew even with them they flew again, taking care to remain in sight. There was no two ways about it: they knew where they were going, and they wanted her to follow. The humans climbed up through what seemed to be an endless tumble of stone until the birds checked at the top of the rise and came speeding back to Kel. They immediately landed on every perch her body might offer, feathers raised, quivering.

"Who needs a wildmage when they're saying plain as heralds that they've seen monsters?" Lord Raoul's voice was an almost soundless murmur in her ear. She hadn't even heard the big knight come up beside her.

He motioned her to stay put, got low to the ground, then inched his way to the pile of boulders that formed the crest. Three of them formed a triangle of space; he unclipped a spyglass from his belt, opened it, and thrust it into the triangle. After a few minutes he closed the glass and worked his way down from his vantage point. With hand signals he urged their party to fall back.

At last he signaled a halt. The men and pages drew close to hear what he'd seen. He rubbed a hand across his mouth for a moment, then said, "There may be more in a cave I saw, but—rough count—I make it about twenty of the things. I'm guessing most are here, now that dark's coming on and we didn't spot any out raiding today. They've laired up in a pocket valley on the far side of that rise. There's a waterfall at the northwest end. It forms a stream that runs out in two branches, east and southeast. It leaves about thirty feet of open ground in front of that cave. There's trees and more rock on the north and northeast sides of the valley—the cave's part of that rock."

He looked at the local guide. "It's Lady's Fall, sir," the man told him. "The gentry picnic there sometimes. The cave's big enough that young'uns feel bold explorin' it, but it's no warren. They can be bottled up in there."

"What of the valley itself? Are there other approaches than the one we just took?" asked Qasim.

"There's a rock stair carved by the fall," said their guide. "We can take a woodcutter's road to reach it without entering the valley. Have they put webs on the rocks around the fall?" Lord Raoul shook his head. "Then mebbe they don't know about the stair. It's slippery, and it's hid well. And there's a deer trail across the fork in the stream. It runs past where we left your soldiers, my lord."

Lord Raoul nodded. "Let's get them. Time to go to work."

Two mages of the Own set up magical shields that would hide them from spidren detection as long as everyone stayed in one spot. Once that was done, the leaders of the force worked out their attack. As they did, Kel looked at the map Lord Raoul had drawn in the mud. The spidrens had picked their camp well. A broad, deep stream lay across the front of their cave, which was set in rocky hills and thick woods. The Knight Commander drew lines to show where the creatures had spun webs and stretched them across the gaps between trees. Some of the soldiers had sacks of a powder that would melt the spidren webs. Once the element of secrecy was lost, the humans could also light torches to defend themselves from attack and from the webs.

Lord Raoul's scouting party ate as the plans were laid. Kel's bread tasted like wood, the thick, cold slices of ham like greasy lead. After Hakuin told them the Yamani proverb "Those who do not eat before battle are eaten by battle," Kel made herself chew and swallow her food. She could not face more than two bites of cheese, and gave her share to Seaver.

"I think I'm going to faint," Neal muttered in her ear.

"Me too," she replied. They smiled weakly at one another.

Once again the party was split up, one group under Lord Raoul, the other under Lord Wyldon. The two lords divided their commands into three ranks. The first was made up of spearmen and mages, the second of bowmen and spearmen, the third of torchbearers and lookouts. Kel, Neal, and the other first- and second-year pages were in the third rank, with one exception. Esmond was placed in the second rank because he could cast bright light.

"He'll see more of the fighting," grumbled Merric.

Qasim overheard. "Depend on it, boy, you will

see more than you want."

Lord Raoul explained how each rank would use weapons, magic, and the torches. Once everyone understood precisely how he wanted things done, he said, "My group will enter the valley from this end, along this branch of the stream." Lord Raoul nodded to the rushing water that ran by the spot where they had gathered. "Lord Wyldon's group will come down that rock stair by the fall and hit them from the opposite side. We meet and push them back on that cave. You lads, we're taking a chance on you, but your training master says you're all up to it."

Even me? Kel wondered.

"I listen when Lord Wyldon speaks, so don't prove him wrong," finished Lord Raoul.

"The third rank, to me," Wyldon said coolly. As the pages and the two men who'd been assigned to help them gathered around, he said quietly, "The torches in your charge are important, but more important still is your task as lookouts. Your eyes must not be in front, toward the fighting, but toward the back. *Keep an eye on the trees, the stream, and the open ground.* If spidrens are outside this valley when we strike, they may attack from behind and roll us up. Do not let that happen. If you see movement, yell, 'At the rear.' The bowmen will listen for it, and cover you."

He looked at them all for a moment, then continued. "The first two ranks will go forward, pressing the spidrens into the cave. *You* stay put. We need you spread out, to give you the best chance to see any surprises." He paused, then said, "What is the warning call?"

"At the rear," they chorused.

"Very well." He looked at each of them, then put his palms together. The pages did the same. "Lord Mithros, grant us victory; if you are merciful, grant it at not too high a price. So mote it be."

"So mote it be," murmured the pages.

"Take a spear, all of you," he ordered. "I don't care what else you're holding, if a spidren comes at you, drop it and get that spear up."

When he went to speak to Lord Raoul, Neal murmured to Kel, "Trust the Stump to have a cheerful outlook. 'Not too high a price,' indeed!"

Kel shook her head at him. "You think we'll get out of this without a scratch?"

"No, but he doesn't have to put the idea in people's heads."

The men were signaling for quiet. The mages were about to remove the wards that kept them hidden. They all gathered weapons and supplies and separated into their groups.

Gods of mountains and the rivers, Kel thought in Yamani, please don't let me bring dishonor to my teachers and my family. She collected a spear.

The local guide led them to the woodcutter's road and onto the waterfall stair. It was cut deep and narrow in the rock beside the fall, which meant Kel never had to look down from a height, only to the next few steps. One thing helped on that slippery descent beside the roaring water: the full moon lit the way. Kel thanked the Goddess, whose lamp the moon was, when she nearly stepped on a section of rock polished like glass by the water's passage. The light showed her the danger just in time.

The bottom of the stair was screened by a tall stand of lilacs. The leafy branches hid them from view in the valley. As they waited, Kel saw Lord Wyldon murmur into the spelled pendant he wore. He raised a hand. The men and older pages of the first rank prepared themselves.

Lord Wyldon's arm dropped, and he led the first wave of their attacking party forward. They ran in silence to fall on the spidrens that lazed around fires by the stream. Something bright exploded high overhead: a ball of the sticky black paste called blazebalm, set off by a human mage. That was the signal for the second group of warriors, archers, and spearmen to run onto the open ground. Behind them came the third rank. All of them, including Neal and Kel, had bundles of torches on their backs and a torch in their free hands. As they ran, they held their torches out to their sides.

When spidrens began to charge from the cave, human mages called on their power. The torches held out by the pages burst into flame.

The two groups of humans came together once more and lined up with their backs to the stream. Now there were human shouts as counterpoint to the shrilling of the spidrens. The boom and crack of magic and the clang of metal against metal added to the racket. A loop of web shot high in the air, glowing yellow-green as spidren webs did at night. Kel saw lattices of the gleaming stuff, potential traps, to her left and to her right. She watched the flying ropes of web until Neal shouted in her ear, "We're lookouts, remember?"

"Oops," Kel said.

Following her orders, she thrust her bundle of unlit torches into the ground end-first, so those in the second rank could grab them at need. She lit them all from the torch she carried, then passed that torch to the soldier in the second rank who reached for it. Turning her back on the torches and the fight, Kel settled her spear in her grip and began to watch the gold-splotched darkness in front of her. The night blindness that came from looking at burning torches took a few moments to fade. Once it did, she saw the ground and trees on the other side of the water clearly. Glancing to her side, she noticed that Seaver watched the fight, not the water or the trees. She nudged him with a booted foot. "Seaver!"

He looked at her.

"We're sentries," she reminded him.

He looked around, gulped, and nodded. Quickly he placed his load of torches, and nudged his neighbor Quinden. He too had forgotten his orders.

Kel had to fight the urge to turn and see how the battle went. Every time her curiosity was about to win, she envisioned the spidren that ate kittens and kept her eyes where they belonged.

From the shouts of the fighters, she knew the

first two ranks were pressing the spidrens back toward their cave. The creatures fought desperately, many armed with swords or axes in powerful forelegs. There would be no surrender; this was a fight to the death.

Kel scanned light-dappled water and shadowed trees. The stream shifted, then bulged. A spidren leaped from the water onto the stream's bank. It carried twin axes.

"At," she squeaked, her throat bone dry. Four more spidrens climbed onto land in the wake of the first. Kel found her voice and shouted, "At the rear! At the rear!"

Seaver turned—he'd been watching the fight again. He gasped when he saw the leading spidren just yards away. His face hardened and he cried, "You killed my father!"

He charged the enemy. The spidren reared on its hind legs to clear its spinneret. Kel knew that move: she had seen it at Mindelan.

"Neal, Merric!" she cried to the boys on either side of her and Seaver. She reached with her spear to knock Seaver's feet from under him. He went sprawling as a loop of web lashed at the spot where he'd been. Glancing to Merric's far side, Kel shouted, "Quinden, all of you! Three steps forward!"

She ran up beside Seaver. The leading spidren dragged back its web, letting it catch on the fallen boy. Kel sensed Neal and Merric come forward as she did, their spears pointed at the foe. Quinden, for all he didn't like her, was just half a step behind.

He and Merric screamed, "At the rear!" when they saw five spidrens were coming at them.

The sight of not one page, but four in a steady line, all armed with spears, made the spidrens hesitate.

Seaver wept in rage as he used his belt-knife to hack at the web that clung to him. He didn't see five crossbow bolts sink into the spidren that had thrown it. The spidren lurched back and reared again, trying to shoot more web at the short line of pages. The tilt of the ground betrayed it, making it tumble back into the stream. Seaver cut himself free just when the spidren's web could have dragged him in after its spinner.

"On your feet!" Kel urged him, kicking his spear closer to him. "Come on!"

Seaver grabbed the spear he'd dropped and lurched to his feet as the other four spidrens charged the pages' line. Kel watched the closest, her pulse hammering in her ears. It came at her with a raised axe in each foreclaw, screeching its fury.

Kel promptly forgot her staff lessons. Holding the spear as she would her glaive, she cut with it in a sidelong arc. The weapon's slim razor point sliced through the spidren's chest and arm, releasing a spray of dark blood. Kel reversed the spear and cut back, dragging the blade down. It bit into the spidren at the neck and stuck there as crossbow bolts riddled the immortal.

Kel had to let the spear go. She looked to either side to see how her friends did. Three attackers lay dead, crossbow bolts sticking from their hides like quills in a hedgehog. One had dragged Quinden's spear from his hand. Merric had cut off the foreleg of another spidren before the archers killed it. One spidren had fallen just a foot away from Neal, its curved sword touching his boot. Neal's spear transfixed the thing, entering at the chest and emerging through its back.

"Neal," breathed Kel, impressed. "Pinned it like a beetle on a card."

"I'm going to be sick," croaked Neal, and was.

"Back into line!" roared Lord Wyldon from the far end of their row. "Get torches if your spears are gone!"

Kel, Neal, Seaver, Merric, and Quinden obeyed.

When the fight was nearly over, the soldiers found they had one more job. Inside the cave was a clutch of more than thirty young feeding on the body of the village woman. None were taller than eighteen inches, but when they saw humans, they rushed to the attack. The men and pages kept them back with their swords until they could roll a barrel of blazebalm into the nest. A mage whispered, and the blazebalm roared into flames.

Hearing the young shriek as they burned, Kel found it was her turn to vomit.

Two days later they returned to the palace, a quiet and weary group. They had packing to do, and one final supper in the mess hall. To the pages' surprise, they were joined by the Shang warriors and the men of the King's Own who had been on the hunt. They all stood by their seats, wondering why Lord Wyldon had not said the prayer and allowed them to sit.

The answer came when the king arrived. As he'd done on the first day of classes, he said nothing before they ate. He dined with Lord Wyldon, Lord Raoul, the two Shangs, and Captain Flyndan at Lord Wyldon's table. No pages were asked to wait on them. Servants performed that task while the pages and the men of the Own relaxed over their food. There was a treat, pies made from the first berry harvests of the summer. Only when they could eat no more did the king rise to stand at the lectern.

"You've had your time of fire," he told the pages quietly. "Lord Wyldon reports that you all did well."

Did he? Kel wondered tiredly. Or did he say the *boys* did well?

The king went on, "I am glad not to have to tell your parents you will not be coming to help with the harvest."

Soft chuckles passed around the room. King Jonathan waited for them to fade.

"You and these warriors did important work, as bloody, dangerous, and frightening as it was. It is the kind of work knights must do in our modern age. You may get thanks only from me, but I hope you know the value of what you did. Go home, now. Laze in the sun and steal apples. Try not to get too out of practice. The realm needs your arms as strong, your hearts as steady, as when you faced those spidrens." He nodded to them and left so quickly that they were still trying to rise as the door closed behind him.

Lord Wyldon came to the lectern. "I know you all wish to pack. Get to it. Keladry of Mindelan, report to my office at the next bell."

"I'm sorry," whispered Merric. He got up awkwardly and fled the room.

"You saved my life," Seaver added, his voice cracking. He hugged her one-armed around the head as if she were one of the boys, and followed Merric out.

When none of her other friends moved, Kel forced herself to rise and pick up her tray. "Have a good summer," she whispered, and took her things to the servants for the last time.

She had thought she'd resigned herself to being packed off for good. From the way her food turned to a lump in her belly as she trudged back to her room, she hadn't done it as well as she thought.

There was a letter from her mother on her bed. With all the preparations needed for Kel's older sisters Adalia and Oranie to be presented when the court social season began that fall, her parents had come to stay at their Corus town house for the summer. They looked forward to seeing Kel there. As Kel read the letter, her gloom deepened. She could not stay in town with her parents and sisters. She might encounter people she knew from the palace. How could she live in the city, watching knights come and go, knowing she would never be one of them?

I'll ask them to send me home to Anders at Mindelan, she thought sadly. They'll understand. It was a good idea, but the thought of the "I-told-you-so's" that her sisters-in-law would hurl at her made her cringe.

Her sparrows were nowhere to be seen as she entered her room. They had rejoined the flock-mates who had stayed behind, whirling around the courtyard to celebrate their return. Now they chattered as they perched in the small tree in the court-yard.

"I'll miss you," whispered Kel. She would ask Daine if she could still take Peachblossom. With two daughters to present at court, her parents would be hard pressed to also buy a warhorse.

Thinking of the birds and Peachblossom, she felt her eyes sting with tears. I am *not* going to let Lord Wyldon see I've been crying, Kel told herself. Fetching her glaive, she did a pattern dance to pass the time.

The dreaded bell finally rang. Kel put her glaive down, combed her hair, and washed her face. Then she walked to Lord Wyldon's office, feeling like a prisoner on the long walk to the gallows.

The servingman bowed to Kel, then opened the door and announced her. She entered the office, listening to the door as it closed at her back.

Lord Wyldon stood with his back to her, staring through a window that opened onto a palace rose garden. Was he looking at flowers, she wondered, or maybe at the nobles who walked there as the skies grew dark?

"You sent for me, my lord," she said.

Lord Wyldon sighed and turned. "Sit down, girl."

Kel hesitated, then sat.

Wyldon absently massaged his right arm. "I want you to listen to me. I speak to you as I would to *my* daughters."

Kel blinked at him, startled. She supposed she knew that Lord Wyldon had a wife and family, but she had forgotten it. It was hard to imagine him with any life other than that of training master to the pages and squires.

"Now that you have made your point, consider the future. Soon your body will change. The things that you will want from life as a maiden will change. Pursue the course you have, and you might be crippled by an accident." He looked at his right arm and smiled crookedly. "What if you fall in love? What if you come to grief, or cause others to do so, because your thoughts are on your heart and not combat? This year was the easiest."

You think so? she asked him silently. It wasn't *your* year, was it? She opened her mouth to reply.

"Not now," he said, raising his hand. "Do not answer me now. Go home and think about it." He sighed. "You are dismissed."

She had to hear him say it. "I can't come back, then."

The training master shook his head wearily.

"Should you desire to return at the end of September, you may do so. I hope that you will choose otherwise."

Now Kel was *really* confused. She stood, her knees trembling. "I can come back in the fall?"

Lord Wyldon nodded. "That is what I said. You may return. Good night, Keladry."

"Good night, Lord Wyldon." Outside his office, she felt a wave of giddiness sweep over her. She turned and pressed her face against the cool stones of the wall.

Back in her room, she reread her mother's letter. Now she was glad the family would be in town. She could visit Peachblossom, ride him—maybe practice what she had learned so as to be in shape for autumn.

She threw down the letter and ran into the hall, trembling with excitement. "Neal!" she yelled. "Roald, Seaver, Merric! I can stay! *I can stay!*"

Two weeks after moving to her parents' town house, Kel returned there from an afternoon spent with Peachblossom. To her surprise her mother met her as she came in. Ilane looked at her, then shook her head. "I'm still shocked by how much you grew this year. You'd think I'd be used to it by now. How much was it? Three inches?"

Kel nodded. "I'm five feet three inches tall now," she said proudly. "Another inch and I'll catch up with Papa."

"He'll be delighted, poor man," said her mother teasingly. "I came to tell you that a crate arrived while you were out. There's no sign who it's from. I had a footman pry off the lid, but no one has touched it."

Kel ran up to her room. A large crate filled with heaps of wood shavings waited there for her. Kel worked her way through the shavings until her fingers bumped against something large, wrapped in cloth.

"Well?" asked Ilane.

Kel turned. Both her parents stood in the doorway, looking as puzzled as she felt. "I think I need help getting it out," she said.

Piers came over. Between them, he and Kel wrestled a bulky, heavy parcel wrapped in oiled cloth out of the crate. The minute Kel saw its rough shape, she guessed what it was. Her heart drummed in her chest. Using her belt-knife, she cut away the cords that held the cloth around the thing.

It was a saddle—not just any saddle, but a tilting saddle, made high in the front and back. It was dark wood with brown leather fittings, but the workmanship was beautiful, the materials the finest that could be had. She ran her fingers over the padding, feeling how soft it was.

"And there's no message of any kind?" demanded Ilane. "It's such an expensive gift! Not a note? Has anyone mentioned sending you a present?"

As she and her father searched for a note, Kel told them about her belt-knife and the bruise balm. When the crate produced nothing but wood shavings, she decided to take one more look at the saddle itself. This time she did it with her fingers, exploring each bump and crevice. When she pressed a stud set on the top rim, squarely at the center, she heard a click. A section of the wooden rim flipped up. The girl saw a bit of white parchment inside and drew it out with two fingers. On it was written, "Goddess bless, lady page."

CAST OF CHARACTERS

Adalia of Mindelan	Kel's 17-year-old sister
Alanna of Pirate's Swoop and Olau	the King's Champion, also called the Lioness, born Alanna of Trebond
Anders of Mindelan	Kel's oldest brother, a knight
Baird of Queenscove, Duke	chief of Tortall's healers, Neal's father
Balcus Starsworn	springtime god
Bonedancer	living archaeopteryx (dinosaur bird) skeleton
Chisakami, Princess	daughter of the Yamani emperor, betrothed to Prince Roald
Cleon of Kennan	page in his third year
Conal of Mindelan	Kel's third-oldest brother, a knight
Eda Bell	the Wildcat of the Shang order of fighters
Esmond of Nicoline	new page, starts the same year as Kel
Faleron of King's Reach	second-year page, Merric's cousin
Flyndan	captain, second in command of the King's Own

Gareth of Naxen, Duke	called "the Elder," king's counsellor, training master in Alanna's time
Garvey of Runnerspring	third-year page
Gower Isran	gloomy servant in the pages' wing
Hakuin Seastone	the Horse of the Shang order of fighters
Ilane of Mindelan, Baroness	Kel's mother
Inness of Mindelan	Kel's second-oldest brother, a knight
Ivor	Mithran priest, teaches mathematics
Jasson of Conté	youngest prince
Jonathan of Conté	King of Tortall
Joren of Stone Mountain	handsome third-year page
Kaddar Iliniat	emperor of Carthak
Kalasin of Conté	oldest princess
Keladry of Mindelan	known as Kel, ten-year-old daughter of Piers and Ilane of Mindelan, first female page candidate
Liam of Conté	younger prince
Lianne of Conté	youngest princess
Lindhall Reed	mage, biology teacher
Merric of Hollyrose	new page, starts the same year as Kel, Faleron's cousin

Myles of Olau, Baron	Alanna's adoptive father, teacher, head of royal intelligence service (spies)
Nariko	Yamani armsmistress/ teacher at the imperial court
Nealan of Queenscove	Kel's sponsor, called Neal, son of Duke Baird
Numair Salmalín	mage, born Arram Draper
Obafem Ezeko	sergeant, trainer from the Tortallan army, formerly from Carthak
Oranie of Mindelan	Kel's sixteen-year-old sister
Piers of Mindelan, Baron	Kel's father, diplomat
Qasim	Bazhir soldier in the King's Own
Quinden of Marti's Hill	new page, starts the same year as Kel
Raoul of Goldenlake and Malorie's Peak, Lord	knight commander of the King's Own
Roald of Conté, Prince	heir to the Tortallan throne
Salma Aynnar	head of servants in the pages' wing
Seaver of Tasride	new page, starts the same year as Kel

Stefan Groomsman	Chief Hostler, has wild magic with horses
Thayet of Conté	Queen of Tortall, commander of the Queen's Riders
Tilaine of Mindelan	Kel's sister-in-law, Anders's wife
Timon Greendale	headman of palace servants
Tkaa	basilisk, immortal, teaches magic to the pages
Upton Oakbridge	palace master of ceremonies
Veralidaine Sarrasri	known as Daine, called the Wildmage
Vinson of Genlith	third-year page, Joren's crony
Wyldon of Cavall, Lord	training master of the pages and squires
Yayin	Mithran priest, teaches reading and writing
Zahir ibn Alhaz	third-year page, Bazhir

GLOSSARY

Balor's Needle: a tower, the highest part of the royal palace in Corus, used mostly by astronomers and mages.

basilisk: immortal that resembles a seven-foot-tall lizard, with slit-pupiled eyes that face forward and silver talons. It walks upright on its hind feet. Its hobby is travel; it loves gossip and learns languages easily. It possesses some magical skills, including a kind of screech that turns people to stone.

Bazhir: the collective name for the nomadic tribes of Tortall's Great Southern Desert.

blazebalm: a thick, sticky substance like paste, which burns when lit (either manually or at a distance) by a mage or archer with fire arrows.

Carthak: the slaveholding empire that includes all of the Southern Lands, ancient and powerful, a storehouse of learning, sophistication, and culture. Its university was at one time without a rival for teaching. Its people reflect the many lands that have been consumed by the empire, their colors ranging from white to brown to black. Its former emperor Ozorne Tasikhe was forced to abdicate when he was turned into a Stormwing (and later killed). He was succeeded by his nephew Kaddar Iliniat, who is still getting his farflung lands under control.

centaur: immortal shaped like a human from the waist up, with the body of a horse from the waist down. Like humans, centaurs can be good, bad, or a mixture of both.

Code of Ten: set of laws that form the basis of government for most of the Eastern Lands.

Copper Isles: slaveholding island nation to the south and west of Tortall. The Isles' lowlands are hot, wet jungles, their highlands cold and rocky. Traditionally their ties are to Carthak rather than Tortall, and their pirates often raid along the Tortallan coast. There is a strain of insanity in their ruling line. The Isles hold an old grudge against Tortall, since one of their princesses was killed there the day that Jonathan was crowned.

coromanel: a flat, crown-shaped piece fitted over the tip of a lance. It spreads the power of a lance's impact in several directions, to make the force less severe.

Corus: the capital city of Tortall, located on the northern and southern banks of the Oloron River. Corus is the home of the new royal university as well as the royal palace.

Domin River: runs through fief Mindelan.

dragon: large, winged lizard-like immortal capable of crossing from the Divine Realms to the mortal ones and back. Dragons are intelligent, possess their own magic, and are rarely seen by humans.

Eastern Lands: name used to refer to those lands north of the Inland Sea and east of the Emerald Ocean: Scanra, Tortall, Tyra, Tusaine, Galla, Maren, Sarain.

Galla: the country to the north and east of Tortall, famous for its mountains and forests, with an ancient royal line. Daine was born there.

Gift, the: human, academic magic, the use of which must be taught.

glaive: a pole arm including a four- or five-foot staff capped with a long metal blade.

Great Mother Goddess: the chief goddess in Tortallan pantheon, protector of women; her symbol is the moon.

griffin: feathered immortal with a cat-like body, wings, and a beak. The males grow to a height of six and a half to seven feet tall at the shoulder; females are slightly bigger. No one can tell lies in a griffin's vicinity (a range of about a hundred feet).

hurrok: immortal shaped like a horse with leathery bat-wings, claws, and fangs.

Immortals War: a short, vicious war fought in the spring and summer of the thirteenth year of Jonathan's and Thayet's reign, named that for the number of immortal creatures that fought, but also waged by Carthakis (rebels against the new Emperor Kaddar), Copper Islanders, and Scanran raiders. These forces were defeated by the residents of the Eastern Lands, particularly Tortall, but recovery is slow.

King's Council: the monarch's private council, made up of those advisers he trusts the most.

King's Own: a cavalry/police group answering to the king, whose members serve as royal body-guards and as protective troops throughout the realm. Their knight commander is Lord Sir Raoul of Goldenlake and Malorie's Peak. The ranks are filled by younger sons of noble houses, Bazhir, and the sons of wealthy merchants.

K'mir, K'miri: the K'mir are the matriarchal, nomadic tribes of the mountains in Sarain. They herd ponies and are ferocious warriors and riders. The Saren lowlanders despise the K'mir and are continuously at war with them. There is a small, growing population of them in Tortall, where Queen Thayet is half K'mir and a number of the Queen's Riders are also of K'miri descent.

mage: wizard.

Maren: large, powerful country east of Tortall, the grain basket of the Eastern Lands, with plenty of farms and trade.

Midwinter Festival: a seven-day holiday center-ing around the longest night of the year and the sun's rebirth afterward. Gifts are exchanged and feasts held.

Mithros: chief god in Tortallan pantheon, god of war and the law; his symbol is the sun.

ogre: immortal with aqua-colored skin, shaped like a human, from ten to twelve feet in height.

Oloron River: its main sources are Lake Naxen and Lake Tirragen in the eastern part of Tortall; it flows through the capital, Corus, and into the Emerald Ocean at Port Caynn.

pole arm: any weapon consisting of a long wooden staff or pole capped by a sharp blade of some kind, including spears, glaives, and pikes.

Queen's Riders: a cavalry/police group charged with protecting Tortallans who live in hard-to-reach parts of the country. They enforce the law and teach local residents to defend themselves. They accept both women and men in their ranks, unlike the army, the navy, or the King's Own. Their headquarters is between the palace and the Royal Forest. Queen Thayet is the commander; her second in command, Buriram Tourakom, governs the organization on a day-to-day basis.

quintain: a dummy with a shield mounted on a post. One outstretched "arm" is weighted with a sandbag, while the other is covered by the shield. The object in tilting at a quintain is to strike the shield precisely, causing the dummy to pivot 180°. The jouster can then ride by safely. Striking the dummy anywhere but the target circle on the shield causes the dummy to swing 360°, so the sandbag wallops the passing rider.

rowel: a star-shaped revolving piece on a spur, which cuts into a horse to get it to pick up its speed.

Scanra: country to the north of Tortall, wild, rocky, and cold, with very little land that can be farmed. The Scanrans are masters of the sea and are feared anywhere there is a coastline. They also frequently raid over land.

Shang: an order of Yamani warriors, mostly commoners, whose principal school is in northern Maren. They specialize in hand-to-hand combat.

Southern Lands: another name for the Carthaki Empire, which has conquered all of the independent nations that once were part of the continent south of the Inland Sea.

spidren: immortal whose body is that of a furred spider four to five feet in height; its head is that of a human, with sharp, silvery teeth. Spidrens can fight with weapons. They also use their webs as weapons and ropes. Spidren web is gray-green in color and it glows after dark. Their blood is black, and burns like acid. Their favorite food is human blood.

Stormwing: immortal with a human head and chest and the legs and wings of birds, with steel feathers and claws. Stormwings have sharp teeth, but use them only to add to the terror of their presence by tearing apart bodies. They live on human fear and have their own magic; their special province is that of desecrating battlefield dead.

tauros: seven-foot-tall immortal, male only, that has a bull-like head with large teeth and eyes that point forward (the mark of a predator). It is reddish-brown, human-like from the neck down, with a bull's splayed hooves and tail. It preys on women and girls.

Temple District: the religious quarter of Corus, between the city proper and the royal palace, where the city's largest temples are located.

Tortall: the chief kingdom in which the Alanna, Daine, and Keladry books take place, between the Inland Sea and Scanra.

Tusaine: A small country between Tortall and Maren. Tortall went to war with Tusaine in the years Alanna the Lioness was a squire and Jonathan was crown prince; Tusaine lost.

Tyra: a merchant republic on the Inland Sea between Tortall and Maren. Tyra is mostly swamp, and its people rely on trade and banking for an income.

warhorse: a larger horse or greathorse, trained for combat—the mount of an armored knight.

wildmage: a mage who deals in wild magic, the kind of magic that is part of nature. Daine Sarrasri is often called the Wildmage, for her ability to communicate with animals, heal them, and shapeshift.

wild magic: the magic that is part of the natural world. Unlike the human Gift, it cannot be drained or done away with; it is always present.

Yama: chief goddess of the Yamani pantheon, goddess of fire, who created the Yamanis and their islands.

Yamani Islands: island nation to the north and west of Tortall and the west of Scanra, ruled by an ancient line of emperors, whose claim to their throne comes from the goddess Yama. The country is beautiful and mountainous. Its vulnerability to pirate raids means that most Yamanis get some training in combat arts, including the women. Keladry of Mindelan lived there for six years while her father was the Tortallan ambassador.

ACKNOWLEDGMENTS

Acknowledgments for this book, and this new series, reach back over years. I owe a debt of gratitude to Jean Karl and Claire Smith, who oversaw the publication of the first eight books set in Tortall, and made me think I might have a few more Tortallan stories still in me. My gratitude also goes to Mallory Loehr and Craig Tenney, who did so much to bring about this latest installment in my burgeoning history of the Eastern Lands.

I would also like to thank the kids who attended my appearance at the San Ramon Public Library in San Ramon, California, one nice fall day in 1995, who made me realize that I should stop thinking about Kel's story and write it; and my online fans, including the loyal members of my AOL fan club, whose eagerness for Kel's story buoyed me up through a long, exhausting year.

For my Spouse-Creature, Tim, our buddy Raquel, and my e-friend Rick, my gratitude for all the support, encouragement, ideas, and last-minute reads and fixes, without which I might not have what sanity I yet possess. I would also like to express gratitude to Eyewitness Books for wonderful research books with pictures, and to the cast and crew of *The X-Files* and the movie *Pump Up the Volume*, for providing me with rich sources of ideas.

Lastly and most profoundly, this is for Kelly Riggio. I'm sorry you had to wait so long for it, and I hope it is worth the wait.

*Turn the page
for an excerpt from* **Tamora Pierce's**
second Protector of the Small *book*

PAGE

Available from Laurel-Leaf Books

PAGE KELADRY

F all that year was warm. Heat lay in a blanket over the basin of the River Olorun, where the capital of Tortall covered the banks. No breath of air stirred the pennants and flags on their poles. The river itself was a band of glass, without a breeze anywhere to ruffle its shining surface. Traffic in the city moved as if the air were thick honey. No one with sense cared to rush.

Behind the royal palace, eleven-year-old Keladry of Mindelan stared at the rising ground that led from the training yards to the pages' wing and decided that she had no sense. She felt as if she'd let people beat her with mallets all morning. Surely it was too hot for her to do as she normally did—run up that hill to reach her rooms and bathe. After all, she would be the only one to know if she walked today.

Who would think this cursed harness would make

such a difference? she wondered, reaching under her canvas practice coat to finger broad leather straps. At some point during her first year as page, she had learned that second-, third-, and fourth-years wore weighted harnesses, and that more weights were added every four months, but she had never considered it in terms of herself. Now she wished that she had donned something of the kind in the empty summer months, when she made the daily trek to the palace to keep up her training. If she had, she wouldn't ache so much now.

She wiped her sleeve over her forehead. It's not even like you're carrying a lot of weight, she scolded herself. Eight little disks—maybe two pounds in lead. You trained last year and all summer with lead-weighted weapons, just to build your strength. This can't be *that* different!

But it was. Hand-to-hand combat, staff work, archery, and riding took extra effort with two pounds of lead hanging on her shoulders, chest, and back. I've got to run, she told herself wearily. If I don't move soon, I'll be late to wash and late to lunch, and Lord Wyldon will give me punishment work. So heat or no, I have to go up that hill. I may as well run it.

She waited a moment more, steeling herself. She hated this run. That slowly rising ground was torture on her legs even last spring, when she'd been running it off and on for more than half a year.

No stranger, looking at her, would have thought this disheveled girl was the sort to cause a storm of argument at court. She had a dreamer's quiet hazel eyes, framed in long lashes, and plain brown hair that she wore cropped as short as a boy's. Her nose was small and delicate, her skin tan and dusted with freckles. She was big for a girl of eleven, five feet three inches tall and solidly built. Only someone who looked closely at her calm face would detect a spark in her level gaze, and determination in her mouth and chin.

At last she groaned and began to trot up the hill. Her path took her behind the mews, the kennels, and the forges. Men and women in palace livery and servants' garb waved as she ran past. A woman told some kennel workers, "Looka here—tol' ya she'd be back!"

Kel smiled through pouring sweat. No one had thought that the old-fashioned training master would allow the first-known girl page in over a century to stay after her first year. When Lord Wyldon surprised the world and allowed Kel to stay, many had assumed Kel would "come to her senses" and drop out over the summer holiday.

You'd think by now they'd know I won't quit, she thought as she toiled on up the hill.

She was lurching when she reached the kitchen gardens, her shortcut to the pages' wing. There she had to catch her breath. An upended bucket did for a seat. She inhaled the scents of marjoram, sage, and thyme, massaging her calf muscles. For the hundredth time she wished she could use the palace baths as the boys did, instead of having to go all the way to her room to wash up.

"Hi! You!" cried a male voice from the direction of the kitchens. "Come back with those sausages!"

Kel got to her feet. A cook raced out of the kitchen, waving a meat cleaver. Empty beanpoles, stripped after the harvest, went flying as he crashed through them. Metal flashed as the cleaver chopped through the air. The man doubled back and ran on, plainly chasing something far smaller than he. Once he stumbled; once he dropped the cleaver. On he came, cursing.

The dog he pursued raced toward Kel. A string of fat sausages hung from his jaws. With a last burst of speed, the animal ducked behind Kel.

The cook charged them, cleaver raised. "I'll kill you this time!" he screeched, face crimson with fury.

Kel put her hands on her hips. "Me or the dog?"

"Out of the way, page!" he snarled, circling to her left. "He's stolen his last meal!"

As she turned to keep herself between the man and his prey, Kel glanced behind her. The dog huddled by her seat, gobbling his catch.

"Stop right there," Kel ordered the man.

TAMORA PIERCE captured the imagination of readers more than twenty years ago with *Alanna: The First Adventure*. As of September 2006 she has written twenty-four books. That number includes three completed quartets—the Song of the Lioness, The Immortals, and Protector of the Small—and two Trickster books, set in the fantasy realm of Tortall. She has also written the Circle of Magic and The Circle Opens quartets, as well as a stand-alone Circle title, *The Will of the Empress*. Her books have been translated into many different languages, and some are available on audio from Listening Library and Full Cast Audio.

Tamora Pierce's fast-paced, suspenseful writing and strong, believable heroines have won her much praise: *Emperor Mage* was an ALA Best Book for Young Adults, *The Realms of the Gods* was listed as an "outstanding fantasy novel" by *Voice of Youth Advocates*, *Squire* (Protector of the Small #3) was an ALA Best Book for Young Adults, and *Lady Knight* (Protector of the Small #4) debuted at #1 on the *New York Times* bestseller list. *Trickster's Choice* spent a month on the *New York Times* bestseller list and was an ALA Best Book for Young Adults. The sequel, *Trickster's Queen*, was a *New York Times* bestseller, as was *The Will of the Empress*. An avid reader herself, Ms. Pierce graduated from the University of Pennsylvania. She has worked at a variety of jobs and has written everything from novels to radio plays. Along with writer Meg Cabot (The Princess Diaries series), she cofounded SheroesCentral.com, a discussion board about female heroes; remarkable women in fact, fiction, and history; books; current events; and teen issues. Though she no longer sponsors Sheroes Central and Sheroes Fans, as she did for five years, she is still a devoted member of the sites.

Tamora Pierce lives in Syracuse, New York, with her husband, Tim, a writer, Web page designer, and Web administrator. They are currently cowriting a female superhero, White Tiger, for Marvel Comics. They share their home with five cats, two birds, and various freeloading wildlife.

For more information, visit her at www.tamorapierce.com.

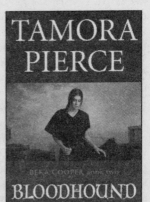